STAGE FRIGHT

A.C. JETT

Questions/comments? The author can be contacted at AuthorACJett@gmail.com.

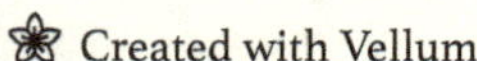 Created with Vellum

1

───────

On a coastal night, the highway lay barren of traffic, but the parking lot of a particular piano bar was jam-packed. Cars, vans, RVs, and even skateboards took up every available space. Inside, the pulsating rhythm of a Russian bear dance tune echoed. The music ended abruptly, earning a thunder of applause.

As the applause died, a pair of hands shifted over a piano keyboard and began a slow romantic ballad.

"I love you so very much, and you will never know why. You mean so much to me that sometimes I must cry. -- Even my mother cries sometimes," a voice belonging to Frank sang. This remark earned a few chuckles from the crowd. Frank paused to roll up his sleeves, exposing more of his arms.

"My star is with me wherever I go, always there in the sky even when you don't show," he admitted, "I try. But I just can't." And the audience could see why: not only was Frank's mouth full of bubble gum, but his singing voice wasn't exactly pleasant. Nevertheless, he was endearing in his own right. Under thirty, with a straightforward look, he radiated a simple kind of warmth. The kind that would make him the first to show up when you needed help.

"...and I love you every day, and I love you every night. So, this loves for you, even when you don't show," he continued, "...cause this love's for you. This love's for you." Frank leaned against the back of his chair, reminiscent of a famous singer. The stage lights began their slow descent into darkness.

Suddenly, the lights went out completely.

"Hey! Hey, what are you doing? I'm singing my song, and you're shutting me off. What are you doing that for?" Frank protested.

"Closing up," a husky voice responded from the bar.

"Yeah, but I'm not done. The audience is still here, right? They want to hear me finish. Don't you? Huh?" Frank questioned, addressing the audience directly.

The crowd responded with brief applause and a few shouts, urging him to continue.

"They always do this to me," Frank sighed, "I take too long on the last set, and they shut me down. Don't know good music when they hear it."

In the dim light, two men sat together at a table. One was pudgy, Fox, wearing a fisherman's hat that concealed an eye, and the other, Ace, was a bearded man with a sharper look. They both carried an air of menace – they were there with a purpose, watching Frank intently, being paid to do so.

Undeterred by the abrupt end to his lighting, Frank announced, "Doesn't bother me. I can sing in the dark. I know what I'm playing. Where was I? My star is with me wherever I go. That's it."

And he resumed, "My star is like the morning dew. It's not far from me. You better believe it. Cause this love's for you. This star's for you..."

Then, as if a lightbulb had gone off in his mind, he retrieved a flashlight from under the piano. It was a double lantern with a white lamp and a blinking red light. He switched both on, placing it on top of the piano. Frank certainly knew how to put on a show.

"My star is with me wherever I go. Always there in the sky. Even when you don't show," he sang, casting beams of light into the shadowy room.

Jessica Blair gracefully entered the venue, her attire suggesting a level of sophistication that seemed mismatched with the laid-back atmosphere of the place. She looked about twenty-five, oozing elegance and style, moving with a confidence that suggested she owned the place. At a glance, the aura she radiated could have been mistaken for arrogance, but anyone who had known her from high school would tell you differently. Behind the glamour was a small-town girl with big dreams.

From the stage, Frank's voice filled the room with his song.

Near the entrance, two burly men, distinguishable as a chauffeur and manager, were on alert, their eyes following Jessica as she made her way toward the stage. The pudgy man and his bearded companion observed the scene with a casual interest.

Frank continued, "This love's for you wherever we go. To see the stars and whisper things, things that you don't know." Suddenly, his voice wavered. His eyes locked with Jessica's. An unspoken history seemed to pass between them. He tried to regain his composure. "Hear me sing 'cause..." His voice faltered again, and the audience patiently waited, picking up on the tension.

Frank's fingers stumbled on the keyboard. He fluffed a bar and started again. Yet, amidst this seemingly embarrassing moment, Jessica gave him a genuine smile that could light up any room. Encouraged, Frank tried once more, his voice slowly regaining its strength. "This love's for all the stars in the sky."

The emotional charge between them was palpable.

"This love's for you. This love's for you," Frank concluded, his gaze still on Jessica.

It was autumn. Fallen leaves littered the sidewalk. The two of them, Frank and Jessica, strolled under the muted streetlights.

"You look good," Frank remarked.

"So do you," she replied with a hint of playfulness.

Frank grinned, "You like my tee shirt? It's got my name on it. Frank. Here. Take a look."

Opening his shirt slightly, he showed her the print.

Jessica smiled appreciatively, "Oh, very nice. I like that a lot."

Frank teased, "You like that, huh? I got another one just like it. Only red with white letters."

Jessica responded, "Sharp. Very sharp."

Frank feigned mock offense, "What's this sharp stuff? Huh?"

Jessica giggled, "You. Hot stuff."

Frank chuckled, "You should talk. Look at you."

She laughed freely, "You're crazy, you know. Same old Frank. Crazy as hell."

Wanting to up the playful ante, Frank gave a playful screech, executed a somersault, and grabbed a handful of leaves, stuffing them down Jessica's dress in a sudden, boyish move.

"Stop. Stop," she protested, laughing, her face a mix of shock and amusement.

Frank quickly apologized, realizing he might have taken the prank a tad too far. "Oh, sorry, sorry. It's all right. My mistake. Sorry."

She just stared at him, the playful indignation in her eyes clear but also a sign she was enjoying the light-hearted moment with him.

In the distance, however, a sleek, intimidating black limousine crept along the road, its lights turned off, adding an ominous undertone to the playful reunion of the two old friends.

2

Under a dim streetlight, Frank skillfully swung around the pole, exuding playful confidence. He looked up at Jessica, trying to read her face. "So what are you doing back in Morro Bay? You scared my audience half to death when you came in, not to mention you know who."

"Well, I was just passing through," Jessica replied, her voice soft and slightly amused.

"Oh yeah? Where from? Mom's place?" Frank asked with a teasing lilt in his voice.

Jessica sighed, "L.A., Frank."

"Do you like it there, Jess?"

She paused for a moment, considering her answer. "Professionally speaking, it's been very good to me."

Frank smirked, "Pretty town. At least it's got that going for it. You singing much now?"

"Yes, some. I've been working with Myron Russel and—"

Frank's eyes widened, clearly impressed. "Myron Russel? Are you kidding? That's like Elvis Presley. That's great."

Jessica laughed, "He's not like Elvis. What are you talking about, Frank?"

"But he's great, right?"

"Yeah, of course, he is."

Frank chuckled, "Case dismissed. Terrific. Working with Myron Presley. That's dynamite, Jessica. Dynamite."

They continued walking until they found themselves in front of Frank's house. Parked nearby was a VW camper, its curtains drawn with trails of cigarette smoke wafting from its windows. Oblivious to the limousine parked a short distance away, the two continued their conversation.

"So what do you say? When are you leaving?" Frank asked, a hint of nervousness evident in his voice.

Jessica looked at him, her eyes searching his. "Are you anxious to get rid of me?"

Frank's expression softened, "You'll never hear me say that." In a dramatic gesture, he stuffed his right hand inside his shirt, imitating the sound of a heartbeat.

She smiled, "Tomorrow morning."

Frank's playful heart pattering halted abruptly. "Why? Don't go. Why do you do this to me? Why do you come back? You know how I get. You come to see what a failure I am, the town clown. Have a laugh?"

Jessica's face took on a serious expression, "No."

"Then why? I still love you, Jess. You're the only one... I do."

"Frank," Jessica began, her voice heavy with emotion, "I'd like to talk. There's something I have to tell you."

"Okay," Frank murmured.

They went to Frank's apartment on the second floor of an older house. The small space contained all the essentials of living, with a piano taking up most of the central area. They sat, finishing their coffee. Frank, now perched on the piano bench, asked, "Want more?"

Jessica shook her head.

"You want some music?"

Again, she declined.

"You want me to talk?"

She shook her head one more time.

Slightly exasperated, Frank asked, "So, what do you want to do?"

With determination and softness, Jessica whispered into his ear, "I want... I want it to be just like before." She kissed him, her fingers reaching for the light switch.

As the light in Frank's flat dimmed, in the nearby VW camper, Fox, identifiable by his pudgy physique, discarded his cigarette out the window. "Well, that settles that," he mused aloud.

Next to him, Ace exuded an air of strength and reason and nodded in agreement. "Let's get some sleep." With that, they drove off into the night.

The imposing black limo loomed large, its engine purring ominously by the curb.

Inside Frank's dimly lit room, warmth and intimacy pervaded. A solitary candle flickered, casting gentle shadows on the walls. Frank and Jessica lay together, semi-dressed, beneath the covers. Their movements were tender—light kisses, soft touches—both careful and considerate, smiles exchanged between lingering glances. Jessica clung tightly to Frank, palpable tension in her grip.

"What's the matter, Jess?" Frank whispered, his voice laced with concern.

She hesitated, taking a moment to gather her thoughts. "Frank? I'm going to miss you so much. I don't know why."

Though Frank was somewhat puzzled by her words, he hardly had a moment to ponder her sentiment. Jessica's passionate onslaught of kisses consumed him. Their mutual excitement drowned out the outside world, including the knock on the door. But the violent kick that followed, splitting the door open, was impossible to ignore. Two imposing figures stormed in, moving with alarming speed. One of them yanked Jessica's dress from the floor as they forcibly separated the pair.

"Hey. What are you doing? What's going on? Give me that. Listen, pal..." Frank attempted to intervene, but his efforts were met with brute force. One of the intruders slammed him against the stove, fixing him with a gaze so intense it felt lethal.

Outside, the night seemed even darker as the two men roughly bundled Jessica into the waiting limo before speeding away. A disheveled Frank stumbled down the front steps, clad only in his shorts. Breathless and desperate, he screamed into the void, "Jessica? Jessica?"

In a nondescript motel room, pacing the floor was Myron Russel. Despite being in his early fifties, he bore the visage of someone much younger—handsome, sharp, and undeniably charismatic. Known for his persuasive charm, Myron had made a career convincing people to bend to his will. But now, he was visibly agitated.

"Get your things together. We're flying out," he ordered tersely.

Tears welled in Jessica's eyes. "I couldn't tell him, Myron. I just couldn't."

"The plane leaves in forty-five minutes. It's a half-hour drive to the airport. We'll talk about it in the car."

"We'll talk about it now, dammit."

"The car, Jessica."

"I'm not going."

Myron signaled to his men, who had been waiting by the door. They exited the room, taking the luggage with them.

"Jessica, if you continue to act like a child, you will be treated like a child. When you act like an adult—"

"Please, Myron... I'm sorry."

"I don't like what you did tonight, Jessica."

"We're different people. That's all."

"You were supposed to tell him the truth but didn't tell him anything. Did you?"

"I did. I told him I loved you," she lied, attempting to defuse the situation.

"Jessica." Myron sighed, pulling her close and pressing his lips to hers. She clung to him, searching for comfort.

"Can we just not talk about what happened? I don't feel very good about it, Myron. I mean that."

"We won't talk about it, baby."

"That's probably the best thing. I thought I could handle seeing him again, but I just can't. He's such a boy, you know. I wanted to see if there was anything there between us. There isn't."

"We won't talk about it anymore," Myron reassured her, leading her toward the door.

"All right. It's over. I see that now. I really do. It's all over, and I'm glad."

3

A school bus bathed in the morning sun. The bus ambled along the winding canyon road, its signature yellow exterior glowing in the morning light. Frank, the driver, was on his usual route, stopping periodically to pick up eager students. At one stop, a young boy, Thad, barely five years old, and his older sister, Gina, who was nine, hopped on. Their bright eyes and lively demeanor immediately set them apart as two of the most vivacious children on the bus.

A singsong chorus began from the back: "Old bus driver, speed up a little bit. Speed up a little bit. Speed up a little bit. Old bus driver speed up a little bit. We wanna geta' school on time."

As the chant filled the bus, Thad, lost in fun, tripped on the steps and scraped his knee. Gina shot Frank a worried glance. Sympathizing, Frank handed her a Band-Aid from his stash. "Don't waste it," he remarked, "It's my last one."

The bus continued its journey until it passed a parked VW camper along the canyon road. Just beyond, a large group of children waited. As Frank pulled over to pick them up, Fox emerged from the camper wearing an odd, gawky mask that covered his face. His quirky appearance evoked laughter from the children, but there was something more to Fox than met the eye.

"All right, all right. Break it up," Fox commanded, wielding a tackle box and fishing rod, "C'mon, c'mon. Get outta my way."

Frank frowned in confusion. "Hey, what are you doing?"

Fox didn't miss a beat. "Problem with your bus. Everybody off. Let's go. Hurry up."

Frank's protective instincts flared. "You can't do this. This is school property. Who are you?"

Spotting Thad and Gina, Fox ordered, "All right, you and you, stay on. The rest of you—off."

Gina mustered some courage to mock Fox's getup. "Big nose, it's not Halloween, you know."

Growing more alarmed, Frank protested, "Hey, what do you think you're doing here?"

With a smirk, Fox replied, "I'm working for Charlie Tuna. You know how to drive this box?"

Frank's confusion deepened. "Who are you?"

Fox revealed a gun without warning and pressed it into Frank's temple. "School inspector. Now drive!"

With the doors slamming shut, the bus sped away, leaving behind the stranded students, who voiced their concerns and speculations about the strange event.

Inside, the bus headed north along the Coast Highway. Fox's intentions remained a mystery. The children, not entirely grasping the gravity of the situation, sat toward the back, discussing their next move.

Frank attempted to reason with the intruder. "You won't get away with this. Not in a million years, you won't."

Fox simply retorted, "I am, though. Right?'

Gina piped up, her stomach growling, "I'm hungry now. Let's stop."

Her little brother chimed in, "Are we skipping school?"

Gina rolled her eyes, "No. We're just going the long way, dummy."

As Thad occupied himself with his toy helicopter, Frank again tried negotiating. "Look, pal. I don't know why you're doing this, but it's against the law, and I'm responsible for what happens here."

Fox's response was cold. "Don't I know it?"

Frank persisted, "So why don't you just let us get off, and you can keep the bus if you want."

Fox teased, "You want to jump first?"

Peering at the road whizzing by, Frank said, "Not at this speed."

But Gina, ever the assertive one, wouldn't be silenced. "Hey, I'm hungry. How come nobody ever listens to us?"

Both she and Thad bounded to the front of the bus. "Is this a hijacking, Mister Tuna?" Gina inquired.

Fox, amused, responded, "Might call it that."

Undeterred, Gina declared, "I don't care what you call it. I want to eat."

Thad nodded in agreement, adding, "Me too. So there."

At the bustling bus garage office, phones rang incessantly, and drivers clocked in for their shifts. With oil-streaked hands, a mechanic approached the supervisor, who looked like he had too many things on his plate.

"Still not back?" the supervisor inquired, brow furrowed.

"Not yet," the mechanic responded, "He must have broken down somewhere."

The supervisor shook his head, anxiety etched on his face.

"No. I checked with the school. The parents. They haven't seen him. I'll call the police."

The mechanic winced, "But the license on that one expired. It's not supposed to be out. They're going to give you a fine, for sure."

With a sharp glare, the supervisor snapped, "Go brush your teeth, Fletcher."

Meanwhile, an A&W drive-in was witness to an unusual scene. Parked awkwardly was the school bus, with Frank and the kids happily munching on burgers inside. Fox stood a little distance away, scanning the surroundings while sipping a milkshake.

With a hint of defiance, Gina asked Frank, "Can't you do something? You're the driver."

"I'm thinking. Believe me," Frank replied, trying to sound reassuring.

Thad, with wide-eyed innocence, chimed in, "I know. Let's just sneak away, and he won't ever see us, and we can drive the bus and go back to school, and that's it."

Frank pointed out the obvious, "He's got the keys."

Thad's face fell. "I forgot."

Gina formulated a plan, "I know. Thad and I could pretend we got sick, and you could take us to the hospital. What do you think about that? What's your name?"

"Frank," he replied, pointing to his name badge.

Gina pressed on, "What do you think, Frank?"

Frank sighed, "I don't know. We got to do something. I have to play tonight."

Suddenly, the door creaked open, and Fox stepped in, "All done? You like it?"

Gina made a face, "Yechhh."

Thad wiggled in his seat, "I have to go pee."

·   ·   ·

Soon after, all four found themselves in the men's room. Gina looked around in confusion, "But this is for boys. Look, Thad. They even have those little bathtubs on the wall."

Thad innocently asked Fox, "You going to take a bath now?"

Fox snorted, "What for? I'm not dirty."

Thad wrinkled his nose, "Then how come you smell?"

Fox shot back, "Hey, you just take care of you, and I'll take care of me, okay?"

Thad hesitated as he approached a urinal, "I can't pee with a girl in here."

Gina teased, "I'm not a girl. I'm your sister. Anyway, I've seen you lots of times already. You've got nothing to hide."

Despite her reassurances, Thad remained adamant, "I don't care. Cover your eyes. Everybody. And no peeking."

Amidst all this, Fox checked his reflection, the gun evident in his belt. Gina tried to sneak a peek while Frank inched closer to Fox, his eyes on the firearm. In a playful distraction, Thad exclaimed, "Look, Frank. No hands."

Suddenly, Frank lunged for the gun, but Fox was quicker. His hand shot out, gripping Frank's wrist tightly.

"Don't be stupid, kid," Fox growled, "Nobody's supposed to get hurt here."

Desperation was evident in Frank's voice, "Look, these are just kids. Why don't you let them go? Keep the bus. I'll take you wherever you want. Anything. Whatever. Just let them go, alright?"

Fox's laughter was devoid of humor, "You don't understand too good, do you, Franco? It's not you or the lousy bus we want. It's the kids."

Back on the road, the bus continued its journey, with Fox meticulously cleaning his fishing lures. Gina and Thad whispered amongst themselves while Frank grappled with the uncertainty of their predicament.

Gina suddenly piped up, "Hey, we don't have to go back right now. It's Friday afternoon."

Frank's concern was evident, "But what about your mom?"

Gina shrugged, "What about her?"

"She'll be worried sick," Frank pointed out.

Thad, with a hint of bitterness, interjected, "She's a bitch."

Frank reprimanded him, "Hey, you don't talk like that about your mother."

Gina smirked, "Why not? She does."

Thad mused, "Yeah, but Dad doesn't. Let's go see him. He's more fun than Mom."

Gina nodded in agreement, "Yeah, let's. We can go fishing, and I know where. It's not that far, Frank. Mom won't care."

Thad's eyes gleamed with excitement, "Yeah! We're going fishing."

Frank's response was firm, "Forget it. Hey, there's no way. Just forget it. Alright! I'm taking you back, and I'm getting me back."

Fox approached them with a grin, and Thad cheerfully asked, "Hey. Let's fish. You want to, mister?"

Fox's response was nonchalant, "Sure. Got time to kill. Might catch some later. I'd like that. What about you, sport?"

Frank was having none of it, "Not interested."

Fox feigned confusion, "Why not? It's fun. You don't like fun?"

Frank retorted, "Look, I don't know what kind of game you're playing, but I don't like it any way you say it. You can't just go around hijacking buses and making us do things against our will. They're going to find out we're gone, and when they do, they'll nail you to the wall."

Fox's voice took on a chilling tone, "Relax, kid. Relax. This is no game. This is for real. I know that. They know that. And I'm gonna make you the star."

4

Victoria, B.C., shimmered in its glory. It was an idyllic town with boats bobbing on gentle waves, flowers blooming in vibrant colors, the hustle and bustle of double-decker buses, and the renowned Empress Hotel standing tall in its historic grandeur. The hotel was famous for its refined tea service with sugared strawberries and scones fresh from the oven.

Amidst this backdrop, Myron alighted from a jetfoil and entered the hotel.

A portly man of about eighty, Basil Gwither exuded a sense of old-world charm and opulence inside the conservatory. He sipped his tea with the finesse of someone who had dealt with high society's most sophisticated members. His underworld connections, while discreet, were no secret to those who mattered.

"I understand you decided to accept my little suggestion, after all, Myron," Basil remarked without taking his eyes off his tea.

Myron replied, "I never let family ties get in the way of business, sir."

Basil smiled faintly, "No, of course, you don't. That's very decent of you. I trust you still have your engagement in Seattle, then?"

"Tomorrow night. The opera house. I'll save you the best seats," Myron responded.

"You're very generous for a man with no money. However, I must decline. As you know, I run my affairs from this side of the border and am loath to cross it under any circumstances."

"Of course," Myron replied with a hint of mockery.

Trying to keep the upper hand, Basil inquired, "Tell me. Are the jetfoil people still providing you with personalized service off that island of yours?"

"First class," Myron responded.

"Excellent. It's not something you would care to lose, then," Basil mused.

Myron assured, "I don't see that happening. Everything looks too good."

"Fine. We'll be seeing you in a day or two, then. Shall we?" Basil concluded.

"Thanks for the tea," Myron said as he left.

As Myron left, two men approached Basil. The one in the white suit was King, while the other, Earl, sported a finely trimmed mustache and carried an umbrella. The duo was Basil's watchdogs, tasked with ensuring his orders were carried out, often with a touch of ingenuity.

Basil said, "I'm not entirely sure our friend is as competent as he would like us to believe. I've always said that if a man expects to gain anything in this world, he should insure his investments. I have something for both of you to do."

· · ·

A bus trundled towards the renowned San Simeon castle, its pace agonizingly slow. Frank, sitting inside, watched as the bus puttered to a halt, running out of gas. Thad and Gina were having a ball at the wheel, seemingly unfazed by the situation.

Outside, Fox and Frank pushed the bus, trying to gain momentum as they approached a slight incline. The bus began to roll, gaining speed, before finally arriving at a gas station.

The pump man approached, visibly taken aback by Fox's mask. The interior of the bus buzzed with conversation.

"So what are they? Cheap or something?" Fox asked. "No gas."

Frank replied, "I took it by mistake."

"You're telling me," Fox said, sounding annoyed.

Back inside the bus, Thad was engrossed in his toy helicopter.

"But why would he do this?" Frank questioned.

Thad said, "Mom hates us. She's taking us to the zoo."

"The zoo? You know this guy?" Frank asked, bewildered.

Gina said, "Looks a lot like frogman Fisher, doesn't he, Thad?"

"Yep," Thad confirmed.

"How can you take this so lightly? You're being kidnapped, you know," Frank argued.

"Yep," Thad echoed.

"It's happened before. You get used to it," Gina stated.

Frank was flabbergasted, "You're kidding."

Outside, Fox was in a heated conversation with the pump man about the payment. When the conversation escalated, Fox's temperament snapped, showcasing the perilous side of his personality.

With a gun and a devilish grin, Fox declared, "No charge."

The bus roared back to life and continued on its journey.

On the highway, the school bus coasted along, surrounded by the towering trees of a dense forest. Inside, Frank seemed anxious. "They'll be after us for sure, now," he murmured.

Fox, wearing a mask, tried to reassure him. "It's about time. But nothing to worry about, kid. Trust me."

But Frank wasn't convinced. "Trust you? Are you out of your mind? You steal school property, kidnap these poor kids, and almost kill that guy. You expect me to trust you?"

Fox smirked, pulling out an FBI badge. "See," he said.

Frank hesitated before asking in a subdued voice, "Are you really?"

"Who else?" was Fox's pithy reply, his voice laced with an undercurrent of mischief that sent shivers down Frank's spine.

Frank swallowed hard, his voice tinged with disbelief, "But why?"

Fox leaned back, an unsettling smile playing on his lips. "Why not? It only cost me a buck."

Back at the gas station, the situation was rapidly escalating. A police car was conspicuously parked in the bay, the smell of gasoline permeating the air as a pool formed dangerously close to the vehicle's tires. One of the cops casually flicked ash from his cigarette out the window, narrowly missing the pool — for now.

With a valiant effort, the pump man tried to maintain his composure, leaning into the car window to communicate with the law enforcement officers. "You get the license number?" inquired the first cop, his voice emanating a no-nonsense authority.

"No. Look, he can't be more than fifteen minutes ahead of you," the pump man replied, a note of urgency in his voice.

With a quizzical frown, the cop pressed further. "You see the guy?"

The pump man nodded gravely, "He had a mask. You better hurry if you're going to catch up."

The first cop leaned back, skepticism etched across his features. "Well, what color was the bus?"

An incredulous laugh escaped the pump man, his patience clearly wearing thin. "What color was the bus? Yellow. There are no other colors."

With a smirk, the cop retorted, "There are where I come from. Lots of them. — Well, it sounds to me like this Corbin character. We'll get him. Don't sweat it."

Before the pump man could reply, the second cop flipped the siren on and tossed his cigarette out of the window, seemingly oblivious to the danger it posed. The car shot out of the bay with a surge of speed, leaving a horrific explosion in its wake that shook the entire area.

Inside the speeding police car, the two officers exchanged a bewildered look. "What do you suppose that was?" asked the second cop, his voice betraying a note of worry.

"Earthquake. Supposed to be one today," replied the first, his nonchalance bordering on absurdity.

Their conversation was cut short as they sped down the highway, rapidly gaining on the bus where Thad was curiously toying with the emergency exit. With a triumphant yank, the entire door came off its hinges, revealing the pursuing police car to Gina.

. . .

"Hey, Gina. Look. Police," Thad called out, a twinge of excitement in his voice. Fox was at their side in an instant, urgency apparent in his actions.

"Get away from there. You want to get hurt. Come on," Fox admonished, swiftly carrying Thad to the front of the bus.

Frank's voice trembled with anxiety, "We better stop. We don't want any more trouble than we already have."

"Sure we do." Fox dismissed the idea with a cavalier wave of his hand. "It's no trouble at all."

At that moment, the police car pulled alongside the bus, loudly hailing them through the speaker. "Pull this bus over. You are in violation of the law," shouted the second cop, his voice echoing ominously through the speaker.

Undeterred, Fox seized a megaphone and yelled back, "Go jump in the lake!" cunningly keeping out of sight so that the police would assume Frank was the one speaking.

The voice of the second cop blared over the speaker, stern and unforgiving, "You are in violation of the state law. Pull the bus over, or we will be forced to take serious action."

Without missing a beat, Fox taunted back, his voice seething with scorn, "Put your money where your big fat mouth is."

A sense of urgency crept into Frank's voice as he turned towards Fox, desperation evident in his words, "Would you shut up. What are you trying to do?"

.　.　.

From outside, the first cop chimed in, his voice an ominous warning that further fueled the growing tension inside the bus. "Look it, buddy. You're in pretty big trouble. You better pull over."

Undeterred, Fox rallied, his voice carrying a mocking tone that left Frank feeling utterly helpless. "You heard the man, Franco. Pull over."

Confusion was evident in Frank's voice as he responded, a hint of fear creeping in, "What?"

With a sardonic grin, Fox repeated, his voice rising to a crescendo, "Pull—over."

Frank hesitated. He slowly complied with a deep breath that seemed to hold the weight of their fates. But in a swift, decisive move that took Frank by surprise, Fox grabbed the wheel and yanked it with all his might.

The bus lurched violently, sideswiping the police car with a thunderous crash before speeding away, leaving the battered police vehicle in a cloud of dust.

As the bus hurtled down the road, Frank's voice broke through the chaos, a mixture of disbelief and burgeoning anger. "I want to know what you're doing this for. You're not with any police force."

The bus roared onwards, a behemoth bearing the weight of lives at a crossroads, the echoes of Frank's plea mingling with the distant cries of justice trailing behind them. The boundaries of law and madness blurred as the group barreled forward into the uncertain abyss ahead.

As the chase unfolded with frenetic energy, Fox unveiled his reckless determination, engaging in a perilous exchange of gunfire with the pursuing officers. The highway became a battlefield, a deadly dance of swerving vehicles and flying bullets.

Fox seemed to lose all sense of reason, consumed by the fiery spirit of the chase. His shooting grew more precise, even as the police retaliated ferociously. Each shot exchanged only fueled Fox's fervor, pushing him to more dangerous extremes.

Amid the chaos, Fox managed a mocking call to Frank, who desperately tried to maintain control of the veering bus. "Just hold her steady. Easy now."

But as the wooded scenery whipped past, the visibility became increasingly precarious. The police car darted in and out of sight. Yet, their presence was undeniably felt as they continued their relentless pursuit.

Just when it seemed that Fox's reckless actions would result in his demise, a final shot rang out, a bullet from Fox's gun piercing a tire on the police car. The vehicle spiraled out of control, smashing through the guard rail and plummeting over the edge, leaving behind a trail of shattered glass and twisted metal.

In a quiet roadside diner, the humdrum of daily life played out against a backdrop of laminated menus and vinyl seats. Truckers chatted lazily over their breakfast, a Zen monk meditated over his meal, an Esalen runaway flipped through a magazine, and waitresses in pink polyester weaved their way between tables, balancing trays laden with classic American fare. But the stillness was broken by a sudden crash.

A black and white hardtop, sirens wailing, crashed through the roof, landing smack dab in the middle of the monk's club sandwich. Coffee cups spilled, and the waitresses, to their surprise, ended up with egg salad everywhere but on the plates.

The two flabbergasted cops inside the car killed the siren and lights. One looked at the other, wondering aloud, "Maybe we should take the rest of the day off?"

5

Not far off, the bus came to a halt. Inside, Fox smirked, surveying the chaos they had left behind. "That ought to get us some attention," he noted.

Frank glanced back, grimacing. "Yeah, if they're not dead."

"And if they are?" Fox responded with a quirky twitch of his plastic nose, a raised fake eyebrow, and a spin of his colored lenses.

At Monterey Pier, a light fog created an ethereal atmosphere. Fishermen scattered along the pier and cast their lines into the water, hoping for a good catch. However, today's catch wasn't fish but a rendezvous.

Pulling up in a pristine white Mercedes, Pamela Russel, a worried mother, and Howard Stockton, her loyal lawyer, got out of the car. Their purpose? Delivering the ransom demand for Pamela's children, Thad and Gina.

"Are you sure this is the right place?" Pamela's voice was laced with anxiety.

Stockton reassured her, "Mrs. Russel, leave it to me. We'll just do as they asked."

Pamela's fears were evident as she replied, "Any one of these men could just take the money, and I'd never see my children again."

"Most lawyers wouldn't go to these lengths for their clients, but you asked me to, and I agreed. Right?" Stockton said, attempting to placate her.

They tied a hefty bag of money to a post on the pier, ensuring it dangled just above the water line. As they retreated, Stockton advised, "They're probably watching us. So, let's just tie this off and go back to the hotel. You'll have a drink, and we'll wait. Everything will be fine."

As they left the pier, an unassuming fisherman packed his gear. This man, Ace, slid into a brown sedan. Inside, he casually greeted Jack Rose, "Hey ya, Rosie. How ya' doing?" Rose, not much for words, handed Ace a pack identical to the one dangling from the pier.

As the tide receded, the pack Stockton and Pamela had left behind resurfaced. Ace approached in a small boat, claiming the ransom. A seaplane in the distance suggested their getaway. Turning the boat, Ace headed underneath the pier, disappearing from sight, the ransom secure.

Twenty miles south of Monterey, the Coast Highway was a hive of activity. The recent hijacking event generated a tidal wave of publicity, making it a media field day. A helicopter buzzed overhead, closely following the odd convoy: five police cars, a few motorcycles, a TV News mobile, and curious onlookers who had come to catch a glimpse of the spectacle. Leading the cavalcade was the large yellow school bus.

Inside, Frank and the kids sat right up front, their eyes glued to the scene outside, while Fox kept himself hidden behind the second seat.

Frank's voice, tinged with frustration and disbelief, remarked, "They'll probably bring out the Marines next. How do you plan to get out of this?"

With a mischievous grin, Fox, peering out from his hiding spot, responded cheekily, "Who me?" Suddenly animated, he grabbed the megaphone, leaning out the window to shout, "I want to talk to somebody. The news, guys."

As if on cue, the TV van swerved alongside the bus. A camera mounted on its roof captured everything, and a reporter, microphone in hand, asked Frank, "How far do you think you can go with this?"

Frank started, "I didn't do it. It's not my—"

But Fox, not one to let Frank control the narrative, pressed the gun against his ribs, prompting, "All the way, kid. Tell her."

With a pained expression, Frank echoed, "All the way."

The relentless reporter shot back another question, "What if the police don't cooperate with you? What will happen to the children?"

Frank tried again, "Listen, I'm not—"

The gun's pressure became even more insistent.

Fox whispered forcefully, "Kill them."

"I'll kill them," Frank echoed a hint of desperation in his voice.

From their vantage point, Thad and Gina exchanged worried glances.

"He wouldn't do that, Thad," Gina whispered, trying to convince herself.

"Frank's such a sweet guy," Thad mused, equally concerned.

The reporter pressed on, "Can you tell us why you're doing this?"

Finding a moment of resolve, Frank stated, "I'm protesting the mistreatment of children in this state. It's for children's rights."

Fox seemed amused, "Hey, that's pretty good. You think that up yourself?"

Frank, defiance seeping into his tone, snapped, "No, a bunch of kids told me about it, fathead."

Fox chuckled, "That'll keep 'em going for a while. Probably get you on the eleven o'clock news. Didn't I tell you Fox would get you on TV? And that's only the start."

Surveying their surroundings, Fox decided it was time to make a move. "I think it's time we got rid of the escort. Stop the bus. Block the road."

Grabbing the megaphone once more, his voice boomed out, causing the convoy to grind to a halt. "Awright. Hold it right there. I don't want to see no more cops between here and the other side of Monterey. I don't want to see nobody move for an hour. And if I even smell one of you guys within six blocks of me, the kids' bodies will be coming out the back door one after the other. You got that?"

The cops, realization dawning, quickly conferred before their leader responded, "We hear you. You'll have our complete cooperation."

Fox, still masked by the megaphone, commanded, "Okay. So, you stay put. You call the local police and tell them the same."

"You have our word," the leader assured him, signaling to one of his colleagues, "Harry, get Monterey on the radio and tell them to clear the streets."

A voice echoed back, "Roger."

6

Inside the bus, Fox lounged with an air of satisfaction. This was turning out to be his finest hour.

"Awright, Franco. Let's go," he said smugly.

Responding to his command, the bus revved up and hit the open highway, leaving behind a trail of dust.

Back at the police's makeshift command center, the authorities held a conference. One officer was busy with the radio, another was unfurling a map, and a third was heading back to handle the traffic.

"What are the exit routes out of this place? Let me see the map," the leader asked, a hint of impatience in his voice.

Cop 3 listed the routes, "You've got 101, 68, and Highway 1."

The leader processed this quickly. "Okay, we need road-blocks on those three. This guy's not getting out of town. All that leaves is the air and the water."

A voice from the radio interjected, "We can't block off the freeway."

The leader responded, clearly frustrated, "Sure you can. Just block it off. It's easy."

Cop 3 added, "There's no airfields in this area."

With a smirk, the leader said, "Good. So, all that leaves is the water. We need a boat."

"He could take a helicopter," Cop 3 pointed out.

The leader quipped, "Hey if the guy was smart enough to get a helicopter, he wouldn't need to hijack a bus. What are you? Trying to get a promotion or something? Come on, help me out. We need a boat."

A motorcycle cop chimed in, "Are we moving in now?"

Cop 3 reminded him, "He said an hour."

The leader was firm, "Fifteen minutes. That's all he gets. You take that other road to the pier. There's a Holiday Inn right near there. Let us know what he's doing, and I'll try to get us some water power."

With that, the motorcycle cop was off.

The bus meandered through the streets of Monterey. The town was eerily quiet, save for the faint whir of a helicopter tracing its path above.

Fox squinted at the helicopter, "I wonder if that's those cops."

Frank teased, "I thought you said you could smell them."

"Give me a break," Fox retorted, "That's more than six blocks."

Thad joined in the banter, "No. Frank's right. You should be able to smell them." He mimicked the helicopter, swooping his hand right past Fox's face.

. . .

Near the Holiday Inn, the motorcycle cop parked and dismounted, watching the pier intently. There was no activity yet, but his radio kept buzzing with chatter.

The leader's voice pressed from the radio, "What about that boat?"

Another voice responded, "There's only one here, and there's no one to run it. You'll have to come down and sign for it."

The leader snapped, "You just make sure it's ready."

"I'll need authorization first," the voice replied hesitantly.

In a nearby lounge, Pamela and Stockton sipped their drinks. The motorcycle cop positioned himself by a window, equipped with a walkie-talkie and a pair of binoculars.

"They're pulling onto the pier now. He's still got the kids with him. There's nobody else around," he reported.

Pamela, panic evident in her eyes, rushed over to the cop, "Those are my children. What are you doing to stop him? Tell me."

Along Fisherman's Pier, the bus came to a sudden halt. Fox promptly shoved his hostages out onto the rough wooden planks.

"You letting us go now?" Frank inquired, trying to gauge the situation.

"The trip ain't over yet, Franco," Fox replied smugly.

Frank tried to maintain his composure for the sake of the younger ones. "Thad, Gina? We'll just do what he says, okay?"

Both Thad and Gina nodded in unison. "Okay, Frank."

Following Frank's lead, they descended the steps to the water level, where a motorboat awaited them. Ace assisted them aboard.

"We going for a ride in the boat?" Thad asked, his voice shaky.

Trying to sound braver than she felt, Gina responded, "Looks like."

Pamela was now peering through binoculars in the nearby Holiday Inn lounge. The motorcycle cop stood beside her while Stockton anxiously hovered in the background.

"I can't see where they went," Pamela exclaimed in frustration. "Are you just going to stand there and do nothing?" She glared at Stockton, adding, "And I pay taxes for this kind of service and protection."

Meanwhile, back on the highway, the leader glanced at his watch. Time was ticking away, and he felt the pressure. "Time's up. We're moving in. Mount up," he ordered. With that, he hopped into his car, leading a procession of vehicles in pursuit.

On the motorboat, Ace smoothly steered the vessel away from the pier. Fox, feeling victorious, checked his money pack. "Get it all right?"

"It's all here. No problems," Ace confirmed. "And you?"

Fox waved off a lingering concern. "Ah, some helicopter show off. But he's gone now."

Thad interjected, "It was the police, right Frank?" But Frank caught up in the tension of the situation, wasn't in the mood for discussion.

With a hearty laugh, Fox bragged to Ace, "C'mon! Let me tell ya, Ace. We scored big. Only a hotshot singer like Russel could afford to have kids like this." He removed his mask, carelessly dropping it onto the seat. Thad, ever curious, picked it up, placing it next to his toy helicopter.

As the motorboat journeyed on, a seaplane came into view.

"Everything set?" Fox asked, anticipation evident in his voice.

"Sure is. I put her there myself," Ace responded.

Frank's mind raced, "What about us?"

Ace looked him over, "You know how to drive one of these things?"

Frank hesitated, "Not really."

Fox chuckled, "Yeah, well, you can take it back, and the cops'll teach you how."

As the boat neared the seaplane, something unexpected occurred. The seaplane's propeller began to turn.

"I thought you said there was no pilot," Fox snapped at Ace.

"There isn't. It's empty," Ace replied, equally stunned.

Suddenly, the propeller churned again, revving up. The seaplane turned and began taxiing towards the boat, but it wasn't just moving - it was gearing up for takeoff at a harrowing speed.

Fox stood abruptly, "Hey! What are you doing?"

The children clung to the boat, eyes wide with terror. Frank grabbed the wheel swiftly, jerking it hard to the right. In the chaos, he knocked Ace overboard, and Fox was soon to follow, plunging into the bay.

The seaplane wasn't done. It circled back, coming at them with relentless determination. Under the threat of the oncoming plane, Frank navigated the boat with frantic desperation. Thad and Gina's screams echoed above the roar of the engines as the seaplane's propeller sliced through the water, mere inches from their boat.

With adrenaline pumping, Frank made a beeline for the pier, pushing the boat to its limit. The plane pursued them doggedly, casting a massive shadow over the small motorboat.

7

In the dimly lit lounge, every person had thrown themselves onto the floor, tensely awaiting the feared aftermath of the recent events. The plane roared overhead. As moments passed and nothing more occurred, the police officers promptly got to their feet and sprinted towards the pier.

By the mooring slips, the officers hurried along the dock, their eyes darting between every slip and shadow. But the boat they were looking for had vanished and was nowhere to be seen. Above them, the seaplane circled ominously, casting its wide shadow below. The police scattered along the shoreline, each officer taking a different vantage point.

Underneath the pier, Frank skillfully maneuvered through the wooden posts. He backtracked to the shore discreetly, quickly disposing of the boat. With Thad and Gina in tow, he cautiously approached the hotel driveway.

A throng of tourists gathered by the entrance, spilling from a bus. TV news reporters were setting up their mini-cams while abandoned police cars and motorcycles littered the lawn.

Frank whispered, feeling the urgency of the moment, "I either get you kids out of here, or I go to jail."

Gina shot back, a hint of mischief in her voice, "So let's go. I hate crowds."

Thad suddenly pointed, "There — Frank."

His finger directed their attention to a motorcycle with a sidecar. Just as they decided to make a run for it, Pamela and Stockton, weaving through the crowd, spotted the children.

"There they are. Thad? Gina?" Pamela's voice was desperate, but her call was drowned out by the crowd's noise.

Frank wasted no time. He fired up the motorcycle and sped into the busy street with Thad and Gina aboard. Behind them, the roar of traffic and the distant chatter of the crowd grew fainter.

Back by the mooring slips, a police boat finally pulled up to the scene. An exasperated leader greeted them, "It's about time." But a motorcycle cop, out of breath, quickly interrupted, "Better forget about the water, Lieutenant. That kid just stole my bike."

The marine cop, looking quite bewildered, stammered, "Hey, what about the boat? Thought you wanted a boat?"

Meanwhile, Frank masterfully navigated through the rush hour traffic on the freeway. With Thad in the sidecar playfully wiping the dust off cars they passed and Gina clutching the bag of money close, they made their way. The thrill of the escape had the children giddy, and Thad shouted, "Faster, Frank. Faster!"

The chase took them up the coast highway, a serpentine stretch of road flanked by dense forests and a daunting concrete median. As Frank sped past a sign warning of the winding road ahead, he could see a motorcycle cop hot on his trail. Navigating between two mammoth oil tankers, he saw the officer falter in his pursuit. Clearly, the risk was too high for someone with responsibilities back home.

As the highway slithered through the trees, Frank led the chase, with the line of police cars trailing behind. But the winding road soon presented a new challenge. Red pylons lined the shoulder, and as Frank clipped them, they tumbled into the lanes, causing further chaos. Another sign ominously announced: OPEN TRENCH.

Pushing the bike to its limits, Frank managed to steer away from an RV but found the edge of the road unfinished. The sidecar resisted his attempts to bring it back into the lane, threatening to throw them all into danger.

In a split-second decision, Frank reached out, pulling Thad onto the motorcycle's gas tank. Just as it seemed collision was imminent, the sidecar was suddenly clipped off. Breathless but relieved, Frank checked on the children.

"You all right, Thad? Gina? You okay?" he asked, his voice filled with concern.

Having become accustomed to the adrenaline of their journey, Thad responded nonchalantly, "Yep."

Gina added, a smile in her voice, "Good work, Frank."

They continued to zoom down the highway with the wind in their hair. But above, the familiar seaplane drone could be heard again, drawing nearer and nearer.

Inside a dimly lit restaurant at San Francisco International Airport, Frank and the children, Thad and Gina, settled into a shadowy corner. The remnants of their meal lay on the table, evidence of their recent escape from hunger.

Frank's face was filled with remorse and worry. "I'm going to lose my job. My career as a songwriter is over. I'll never get this off my record. I'm a goner, and I'm not even twenty-five."

Thad looked at him with a mix of concern and incredulity. "Frank, relax. You're acting hysterical like my mom."

Gina piped up, her voice filled with understanding, "You're worried 'cause they think you kidnapped us, don't they?"

"And they'll put him in jail, too," Thad added with a tone of realization.

"Don't remind me," Frank lamented. "If only I could nail down that Fox guy. He's the one who got me into this mess, and now he's gone."

Gina's eyes sparkled with an idea, "What about us? We could help."

Frank sighed, his face a picture of defeat, "No, they won't believe you. And your mom will still press charges."

Thad smirked, "Damn right she will."

Gina hurried to reassure him, "But Dad won't, Frank. He can help and everything."

"Yeah. Dad's a pretty good guy. We could fly up there," Thad said with enthusiasm.

Frank's brows furrowed in confusion, "Up where?"

"Back home," Gina explained. "He owns an island up north."

"A big one, and they got fish," Thad added excitedly.

Gina's voice softened earnestly, "He can help you, Frank. He knows lots of people, and he likes us a lot, you'll see."

"Yeah, let's go there," Thad pressed. "I can teach you how to drive the boat and everything. Okay?"

"This is serious, you know," Frank reminded them.

Thad grinned cheekily, "Don't be serious, Frank. We're your friends. We won't press charges."

Their conversation was interrupted when a couple of plain-clothesmen began questioning the bartender. Frank's heart raced as he spotted them, but Gina quickly comforted him, "Don't worry, Frank. Dad will help. Trust us."

Frank's anxiety was palpable, "They've probably got my picture everywhere. There's no way out of this, is there?"

Always full of ideas, Thad suggested, "We could switch clothes?"

Frank chuckled nervously, "Thanks, Thad, but I don't think they'd fit."

Thad suddenly produced the bizarre mask, "Wear this."

Later, in the departures area, Gina and Thad showed their resourcefulness by picking up various items from unsuspecting passengers. A scarf from one, a hat from another, a sweater carelessly left on a chair. Amid the hustle and bustle, passengers seemed oblivious as their belongings disappeared.

Frank stared at himself in disbelief in the mirror in the men's room. Decked out in a large straw hat, a bulky orange sweater, a mini-skirt, tights, and high heels, he looked utterly ridiculous. Gina, trying to be supportive, remarked, "You look great."

Frank's voice dripped with sarcasm, "No way. What would people say?"

But fate intervened. As they contemplated their next move, a Sikh entered the restroom, his traditional attire catching their gaze. They exchanged glances, a plan forming.

In the main corridor of the airport, plainclothesmen and security guards scrutinized every face. But they were caught off guard when a tall East Indian figure, draped in white sheets from head to toe, emerged from a service closet accompanied by two similarly attired children. The trio blended seamlessly into the crowd, their faces hidden by veils.

8

In the dimly lit office of "Plane Rental and Flying Lessons," Hank bid his friend Joe goodbye.

"I'll be in Fresno before midnight. See ya around, Hank," Joe said, tipping his hat.

Hank smirked, "Fly your brains out, Joe."

As Joe left, three figures draped in the garb of East Indians stepped into the office. Frank, the tallest of the three, tried to communicate in the highest falsetto he could muster, "Plane?"

Hank, impatient after a long day, retorted, "No, look. We're closed. You got to come back in the morning."

"Morning?" Frank repeated, trying to maintain his falsetto.

"You got it, lady."

"Fly now."

Hank's patience was wearing thin. "There's no way. Closed, you know. Night. No night lessons."

"Ready."

"Listen, India. No deal. We're closed, understand?" Hank tried to emphasize, but Frank had other plans. In a swift move, he pressed what seemed like the edge of a toy helicopter, hidden under his garments, into Hank's ribs.

"Listen, turkey. You get us out of here, or I'll blow a pipeline through your big fat gut. Understand?"

Hank's bravado vanished, "Hey, relax, lady. I'll do it. Okay. Okay. I understand. Sure." He gestured for them to head out.

On the tarmac, they approached a small plane. Frank continued to wield the concealed helicopter threateningly as Joe, cleaning his Cessna nearby, commented, "So you decided to take another twenty bucks after all."

Hank, trying to keep his cool, responded, "Business is slow. Fly by day. Fly by night. You know me."

Frank interrupted with a sharp, "Keep moving."

Once airborne, Frank and the children, Thad and Gina, removed the sheets disguising them. Hank, having seen through their ruse, exclaimed, "Hey. Hey, you're the guy they had on television. The one that kidnapped that entertainer's kids. Russel, uh... Myron Russel. There's a reward."

Frank's voice dripped with menace. "How would you know?"

"Everyone knows. It was all over the TV. The whole thing. The bus, the—"

"You just be careful what you say," Frank interrupted. "The kids are sensitive about that." He glanced at Thad and Gina, who had already drifted off to sleep. "You kids try to get some sleep, okay. I've got to keep an eye on this... punk."

"I guess it's just you and me, then," Hank muttered.

"You guessed right, pilot," Frank replied.

"And where am I supposed to be taking you?"

"Mars. Now keep flying."

For a while, the cabin was silent save for the drone of the plane. Frank, lost in thought, started humming a familiar tune.

Hank's ears perked up. "Nice tune. Catchy melody. You make it up?"

Frank, a tad irritated, asked, "Something the matter?" The silence returned, only to be broken by Hank's observation.

"Pretty touchy for a tough guy."

Frank, sitting up, said, "Hey! I'm tryin' to think. Ya' mind?"

The vast expanse of the night sky glittered with countless stars, their shimmer bouncing off the vast ocean, painting the horizon with a touch of magic. As the drone of the plane continued, its trajectory was clear — heading north.

Inside the cockpit, tension filled the air. Hank's fingers edged cautiously towards the radio, gripping the microphone in his other hand. He glanced cautiously at Frank, whose eyes were shut, steady snores escaping his lips. Seeing his opportunity, Hank turned on the radio, pressing the microphone to his lips to transmit a hushed message.

"S.O.S.—"

Suddenly, Frank's hand lunged, hitting the button and cutting off the transmission. With a swift motion, he snatched the microphone from Hank, disconnecting it entirely from the console.

"What did I tell you about the radio?" Frank hissed.

"You said that—" Hank began, his voice quivering.

"What's the matter? You got a short memory?"

"I thought you fell asleep. I was only testing—"

"Well, you're wrong," Frank snapped, eyes cold and determined. "I never sleep. I can go for months without sleep. So, keep your hands off the radio and your eyes on the sky. Got it?"

Hank nodded quickly, his gaze fixated on Frank's hand that threatened him with the toy helicopter, pressing it ominously against his ribs. "Sure. Sure thing."

· · ·

As dawn started to break, the plane hovered over the picturesque San Juan Islands. A sense of urgency grew from the cockpit as Hank eyed the fuel indicator, now flashing ominously in the red zone.

"Can't go no further, pal. We're running on reserve," he warned.

Frank's eyes darted around, searching. "This is good enough. Which island is it?"

Peking from her seat, Gina pointed out, "The one that looks like a horse's head."

Thad chimed in, "Near the big white tower."

"Yeah, the power plant," Gina added.

Frank's eyes locked onto the location. "That looks like it over there."

Hank's voice held a touch of panic. "What kind of runway they got?"

Gina shook her head, "No runway."

Hank's concern deepened, "So, where should I put down?"

Frank's voice was firm, "You'll find a road, I'm sure."

But Gina contradicted him, "No roads, Frank. It's all trees."

Growing frantic, Hank exclaimed, "I can't land on top of the goddamned trees."

Frank snapped, "Hey, watch your mouth, will ya? We got innocent kids here. Land on the water."

"No pontoons. I can't," Hank protested. "We'll kill ourselves."

But Frank was unyielding, his voice cold and threatening. "So? This is already a matter of life and death, and if you don't put this watering can down, it will be my life and your death."

Hank's tone became desperate. "This is no watering can, kid."

Frank's voice was venomous. "It will be as soon as I spray some bullets through it. Now land!"

From the backseat, in a sudden and startling moment, Thad shouted, "Bang!"

9

———

The plane sputtered alarmingly above the island. It was running on the fumes of its last fuel reserves. The aircraft swooped dangerously low over the tree-tops, nearly stalling before a timely gust of wind lent it a brief moment of reprieve.

Inside the cockpit, panic was evident on Hank's face, his concern for his beloved aircraft palpable.

"Land. Now," Frank demanded.

"I can't," Hank replied, his voice filled with dread.

"Land," Frank reiterated sternly.

Suddenly, from the back, Thad shouted, "Bang!"

Seconds later, the plane skimmed the water's surface, bounced once, twice, and stalled completely. The engine died with a whimper, and the plane careened into the water, tumbling a few times before coming to a disastrous halt near the shore.

Waterlogged and shaken, Frank, Thad, and Gina scrambled out of the wreckage. The water was up to their waists. Hank looked at his plane, nearly brought to tears by the devastation. As they waded to safety, Frank retrieved the money pack.

"Hey, what about my plane? It's a wreck," Hank lamented.

"You're not kidding," Thad concurred.

Frank, showing a hint of mockery, pulled a Band-Aid from his pocket and handed it to Hank. "Here. And don't waste it. It's my last one."

They reached a stunning house a short distance away – a masterpiece of wood and glass that exuded a northwestern charm. The well-kept grounds showed signs of the changing season, with leaves donning vibrant hues. The three made their way toward the home.

"Don't cut the lawn much around here, do they?" Frank remarked, looking at the overgrown grass.

"The gardener always takes September off, Frank," Gina explained.

"Oh really? Must be nice to be that successful," he replied, a hint of envy in his voice.

Suddenly, Thad's attention was caught by a familiar sight. "Hey, look, my swing. C'mon!"

Trying to lighten the mood, Gina asked, "You want to go sailing later, Thad? Frank, do you?"

"We better find your father, I think," Frank suggested. "Listen, why don't you guys go in first and surprise him, and I'll be right there. Okay?"

As the kids excitedly entered the house, Frank diverted to a nearby gardener's tool shed. He quickly surveyed its contents - rakes, trowels, shovels, spades, and more. After a brief search, he located a compost bin, where he discreetly stashed the money pack, ensuring it was well hidden beneath the layers of decaying matter.

·   ·   ·

Thad and Gina rummaged through the icebox inside the house's kitchen, procuring cookies and milk. Their voices echoed slightly in the emptiness. "Dad?" Thad called out. "Daddy? It's us. Thad and Gina. We're here."

Ruth, a stout woman wielding a mop, eventually answered their calls. Her presence in the house was longstanding, wearing the titles of housemaid, cook, and caretaker with equal aplomb. "My goodness. Look who's here. What a surprise," she greeted warmly.

"Hi, Ruth," Gina said with a smile.

Thad echoed, "Hi, Ruth."

"And where is your mother?" Ruth inquired.

"Antarctica," Thad cheekily responded, sending him into peals of laughter.

Ruth, seemingly unfazed, turned to Gina. "Now, Gina dear, tell Ruthie. How did you get here? Oh, your father will be so surprised when he finds out."

Their conversation was interrupted by Frank's entrance. "I brought them. My name is Frank Corbin. I wonder if you could tell me if Mr. Russel is home," he inquired.

"Well, no, he isn't just now, but he should be back," Ruth informed him.

"Do you know when?" Frank pressed.

"Well, not really. You see, he just comes and goes when he feels like it. I must say the man is a free spirit if I may say so," she replied.

Gina smirked, "You just said that."

Ruth chuckled, "Island fever."

Running on a short fuse, Frank snapped, "Are all you guys, comedians?"

Thad simply shrugged. "Guess so."

"Can you tell me where he might be?" Frank continued.

"Seattle, of course. He has a concert opening there tonight," Ruth said.

Frank's urgency was evident. "Can I use the phone?"

Ruth shook her head, "No. There isn't one."

"Well, how do we get to Seattle?" Frank queried.

"How did you come in the first place?" Ruth countered.

"We flew in," Frank said tersely.

Ruth looked at him with a hint of amusement. "With that man who was looking for gasoline? What a mess. That's what I was supposed to be getting. Gasoline."

Growing more exasperated, Frank pressed on, "Is there any other way off the island?"

Ruth nodded slowly. "Of course there is, but try to tell him that."

"You have a boat?" Frank asked hopefully.

"Not a very large one, but I suppose it might do," she said, a glint of mischief in her eyes.

Frank, Thad, Gina, and Ruth rushed to the boathouse. Frank and the kids donned jackets, hats, and sunglasses to shield themselves from the cool air and brightening sun in preparation for the trip.

"Now, he's staying at the Plaza Hotel. Downtown. You can't miss it. Just ask for it when you get there," Ruth instructed, pointing them in the direction they needed to head.

Without much ado, Frank and the kids hopped into the boat. To their surprise, it wasn't just any boat but a jet boat equipped with twin turbines. This powerhouse could effortlessly achieve 60 mph on the water. While Thad and Gina diligently strapped on life jackets, Frank took to the boat's controls, revving it to life.

"Do you think you'll be all right? It's very powerful, you know," Ruth cautioned, an edge of concern in her voice.

Frank, slightly mischievous, quipped, "Is this one the brake?" Before waiting for a reply, he opened the throttle wide.

The force from the boat's sudden acceleration pinned him back in his seat. They sped off, cutting through an early morning mist thick over the open water, its cool tendrils licking their faces.

Back near the house, as Ruth was about to retreat indoors, Hank approached her, the frustration of the earlier plane crash still evident on his face. "I thought you told me you had some gas," he challenged.

Ruth paused, recollecting. "Just a minute. I forgot. Let me get the garbage. I don't want to make two trips if I don't have to." With that, she entered the house and emerged moments later, holding a pail filled with food scraps. Purposefully, she made her way to the shed.

Setting down the pail, she began to search for the promised gasoline. Hank, eyeing the bucket of scraps skeptically, remarked, "What's that for? Saving it for dinner?"

Ruth chuckled lightly. "No, no. That's compost. Let me see. I saw some gasoline around here, somewhere." After searching, she exclaimed, "Ah, here it is." She presented Hank with a gallon can from under a workbench.

However, Hank's hopes were dashed when he shook the can, discerning it was nearly empty. "You kidding? This won't even start the engine."

Ruth remained optimistic. "You never know till you try."

As Hank expressed frustration with an exasperated "Hah," Ruth began dumping the food scraps into the compost bin. "This turns into methane gas, you know. It builds up a tremendous heat and burns all the organic matter to ash."

Hank, growing increasingly irritated, snapped, "So what? I can't get my plane off the ground. You think I care?"

Eager to educate, Ruth said, "Well, you should. Some people use this for fuel. They even drive their cars with it."

Hank's impatience was evident. "How long 'zat take? Months?"

"Well, certainly before the winter," she replied thoughtfully.

Hank scoffed. "You think I want to skate outa here?"

Ruth, undeterred, stated, "Well, at least you'll be able to fly your plane out, and it won't cost you anything."

Hank's voice dripped with sarcasm. "Fat chance! Last time I met a lady on an island in a shed, I married her. So forget it!"

10

———

The jet boat zipped through the mist surrounding the San Juan Islands, weaving in and out of fog patches. Ferries crisscrossed their path, accompanied by the occasional tanker or sailboat. Steam wafted from the water, and shadowy islands stood sentinel, casting an eerie atmosphere reminiscent of a magical kingdom.

Frank, at the helm, narrowly missed a rocky shoal and decelerated as he navigated past some secluded cottages. The serenity of the island was deceptive, for out of nowhere, a powerful force burst from the trees: a helicopter, which had been trailing them, was back.

Its menacing silhouette dove straight towards them, each twist and swoop calculated and frightening. Trying to evade the airborne menace, Frank attempted to take refuge near the shore, but the helicopter seemed to anticipate every move. Trees brushed against the boat's sides as the helicopter bore down on them, its mechanical maw ready to engulf them whole.

Seeing no other option, Frank sped around the island, but the helicopter relentlessly pursued. Spotting a very narrow channel, Frank steered the boat into it. With densely packed trees on either side, the passage was so narrow that urban streets seemed expansive. "We did it. We did it," Frank exclaimed, thinking he had managed a masterful escape.

But the helicopter was not to be outdone. With a display of aeronautical prowess, it tore through the channel, moving sideways, its rotor skimming the water. Frank tried every maneuver he knew, but the helicopter seemed intent on capturing them.

"Who are those guys?" Frank shouted, bursting into the open waters of Puget Sound, trying to lose the helicopter amidst the thick fog.

From above, the chopper tracked their every move. A door slid open, and out stepped Earl, securely harnessed. With an unmistakable boldness, Earl descended onto the boat, trying to seize Thad, Gina, and the money. Frank resisted fiercely, but the confrontation left Earl with Gina in his grasp. The helicopter lifted, taking Gina with it.

"Gina? Gina, come back," Thad called out desperately, but his pleas faded into the echoing roar of the helicopter's engines.

Inside the Seattle Aquarium, marine life swam freely in their artificial habitats. A cutthroat trout swallowed a candlefish while the rest of the aquatic creatures went about their business. The setting was peaceful, a stark contrast to the earlier chaos. Myron and Jessica sat on a bench inside the dome, immersed in their own world.

"Are you happy?" Myron asked.

"Very. You?" Jessica replied, searching Myron's face for any hint of his feelings.

With a nod from Myron, Jessica confessed, "I love you, you know. Do you love me?"

Myron smiled in response, leading Jessica to tease, "You do.

I know you do. You wouldn't be here with me now if you didn't care."

Lost in his thoughts, Myron's distant demeanor worried Jessica. "What's the matter, Myron? Are you here?"

"Yes, I'm very much here."

She probed further. "What are you thinking about? I never know what you're thinking. You never say anything."

"Just dreaming... I don't know," Myron admitted, his tone contemplative.

Determined to understand, Jessica said, "Our marriage won't be like your last one. I'm a totally different person from Pamela, you know that. Don't you?"

"It's not that, Jessica," Myron reassured her.

Jessica, trying to piece together Myron's concerns, speculated, "You're worried about your kids. It's all the publicity. I think it's bad for your image. It could hurt the concert. Do you think?"

Myron, ever the pragmatist, responded, "No. There's no such thing as bad publicity. In this business, it can only help. Remember that. I only wish I could do more."

Suddenly, the aquarium's speaker system interrupted their intimate conversation. "Mr. Myron Russel. Come to the front desk, please. Mr. Myron Russel."

"I'll be right back," Myron assured Jessica as he rose.

She looked at him with a mix of affection and determination. "I can support you, you know. The same way that you used to support me."

Myron caught her loving kiss with a smile, pressing it close to his heart.

At the front desk, a receptionist handed Myron the phone. "Hello?" he said, a look of concern forming on his face as he listened.

. . .

Later, within the Empress Hotel's conservatory, Myron shook the rain from his umbrella and left it by the door. He shrugged off his wet raincoat, seemingly irritated by the relentless storm outside. Raindrops drummed on the glass roof, accompanied by the tumultuous sounds of thunder and lightning.

"Rotten storm you're having. I almost didn't get through," Myron commented, looking up at the stormy skies.

Basil, who had been waiting for him, responded with an air of profound impatience, "Exactly. Things have gotten a wee bit out of hand, wouldn't you say?"

"Nothing's out of hand. I don't know why you called me here," Myron retorted, slightly defensive.

"Have you collected the ransom money yet?" Basil inquired, his eyes fixed intently on Myron.

"Yeah, of course, I have. We got it yesterday. It's under control," Myron answered, trying to sound confident.

Basil's expression grew sterner. "I am afraid you are grossly misinformed. It is completely out of control. Your men are about as reliable as the weather. Fools, blunderers."

"Well, I thought—"

"Never mind what you thought," Basil interrupted sharply. "Just call them off."

"But I have to pay them fifty grand," Myron protested.

"And you have to pay me a whole lot more," Basil countered coldly.

"You'll get it. Don't worry," Myron assured him, trying to stay calm.

Basil leaned in, his tone dripping with disdain. "Quite frankly, Myron, I have good reason to worry. With the way you are bungling your sordid, little plan, it—"

"My sordid plan?" Myron interrupted incredulously. But before he could further defend himself, Basil threw tea in his face in a fit of rage. Myron flinched, momentarily silenced by the unexpected gesture.

"Do not interrupt me. Ever!" Basil seethed. "I pulled you up from the gutter, and now look at you. No respect." He paused for effect. "You, Myron Russel, have resorted to one of the lowest and most banal forms of mock flattery and self-aggrandizement by inviting a media circus into your private affairs. It's all true."

Basil continued his onslaught, "You have raised police suspicions about yourself. You have no idea who these kidnappers really are, and you've even lost track of your own children."

"No. I wouldn't want to do anything to harm them. Nothing's..." Myron began, but Basil cut him off.

"I'm sure you wouldn't. Nevertheless, I presented you with a clean, bloodless plan to redeem your fiscal obligations. Instead, you have turned it into a form of cheap entertainment. The vice with which you are most comfortable, I know."

Myron, visibly overwhelmed, asked, "Well, what am I supposed to do?"

"Get your men out and pay them off. My people will take over from here. Do you understand?" Basil said, his eyes drilling into Myron's.

Myron nodded, swallowing hard.

"Good," Basil concluded, his voice slightly softer. "It's nothing personal, Myron. It's simply good business. That's all."

11

—————

The Seattle Plaza Hotel, a grand circular tower, stood prominently in the heart of downtown Seattle. The rhythmic hum and swift movement of the monorail whisked by the building was a testament to the hustle and bustle of the city.

Frank and Thad hurried into the hotel's opulent lobby, their haste evident in their swift strides. They wore inconspicuous attire: hats, dark glasses, and overcoats that shielded their identities. They swiftly approached the front desk.

"Is Mr. Russel staying here?" Frank inquired, his voice low.

The clerk, a young man with a polite demeanor, responded, "Yes sir, he is. The Crown Suite in the penthouse."

Frank pressed, "Is he in now?"

"Let me check. Your name, sir?"

"Mr. Corbin," Frank replied promptly. "Tell him Mr. Corbin wants to see him."

As the clerk made the call, Frank's gaze darted around the lobby, the weight of suspicion heavy in his eyes. Every passerby and guest seemed to stare right through him, amplifying his paranoia.

"Top floor and turn left, Mr. Corbin," the clerk finally said, hanging up the phone. "Mr. Russel's been expecting you."

Across the expansive lobby, Jessica engrossed in a newspaper, walked purposefully toward the elevator. Oblivious to her surroundings, she stepped inside. Frank and Thad immediately followed suit, joining her in the confined space. Close quarters meant Thad and Jessica stood shoulder to shoulder, though neither acknowledged the other's presence.

"Hey, look. It's you," Thad whispered to Frank, pointing to a section of the paper Jessica was reading. Frank leaned in to glimpse a picture of himself under the headline: BUS DRIVER GOES BERSERK. As Thad started to turn the page, Jessica interjected.

"Excuse me, but I'm trying to read my paper — Frank?"

The voice cut through Frank's focus. Looking up, his eyes met Jessica's. "Jessica?" he murmured, a mix of surprise and recognition evident in his tone.

The two shared a warm embrace, causing Thad to ask, "Who's that, Frank?"

"Frank, what are you doing here?" Jessica questioned, concern evident in her eyes.

"I was going to ask you the same," Frank replied, still reeling from the unexpected encounter. "We're going up to see Mr. Russel. This is his son, Thadeus."

"Frank, you shouldn't be here," Jessica cautioned.

"The guy at the desk just called. He said he was expecting us."

"Frank, you better go. He can't see you now. You don't know what you're getting into."

"But he's got to," Frank interjected, desperation evident. "I have to talk to him. Explain what happened."

"You better not. Just let Thad go up and leave it at that," Jessica reasoned.

"I'm not going anywhere without Frank. Right?" Thad

asserted, looking at Frank for affirmation. Frank nodded in agreement.

Exiting the elevator, the trio navigated the plush red carpeted hallway adorned with opulent gold fixtures, heading towards the Crown Suite.

"You look terrible, you know," Jessica remarked, glancing at Frank.

"Thanks. I haven't slept," Frank replied, weariness evident.

"Frank never sleeps, right?" Thad chimed in, trying to lighten the mood.

"Wrong," Frank retorted, smiling faintly.

"I thought they caught you in Monterey. That's what they said on TV," Jessica recalled.

"I'm here, aren't I?" Frank countered.

"Frank, why did you have to do it?" Jessica questioned, her voice heavy with a mix of disappointment and concern.

"I didn't. Now, can we just go inside, and I'll explain everything," Frank pleaded.

"Frank, Myron isn't here. He's out of town," Jessica revealed, her eyes searching Frank's for understanding. "If you leave Thad with me and leave now, you might still have a chance."

Resolute in his purpose, Frank said, "Jessica, just open the door."

The Crown Suite was opulent and expansive, the kind of room that hinted at the grandeur of days gone by. The decor exuded a royal flair, making the room's emptiness all the more prominent.

As they entered, Thad immediately dashed to the window, his eyes widening at the view. "Just like Disneyland, Frank," he commented, clearly impressed.

Frank glanced around, his impatience evident. "Yeah, just like it. Where is he?"

Jessica just shrugged, her own uncertainty clear. "Like I said, he's not here." Choosing to bide his time, Frank sat down, trying to mask his anxiety. "Then, I'll just wait till he gets back. He has a concert tonight. He has to come back sometime."

She looked at him, her eyebrows furrowed. "I don't understand what you're doing this for. This isn't like you at all."

"Yeah, well, what can I say?" Frank replied, his voice tinged with resignation.

Jessica's gaze lingered on him. "You've changed. You even look different from when you were on TV. Why did you want to talk to the President, Frank?"

Bewilderment crossed Frank's face. "Jessica, what are you talking about? I never said that."

She pulled out the paper, attempting to show him. "But it says right here."

"I don't want to see it," Frank interjected quickly, his voice rising with frustration. "Look, I'm in trouble and need Mr. Russel to help. That's all."

A wave of sympathy washed over Jessica's face. "I feel so bad for you, Frank. Being chased by the police and then jailed. How did you get out?"

With a tired sigh, Frank responded, "Look, I know I haven't slept for more than a day, but I'm awake enough to know what happened. I was never in jail."

"Yet," Thad smiled.

"Are you sure we're talking about the same guy? Huh?"

She shook her head, looking defeated. "I just don't know anymore, Frank."

Desperation evident in his voice, Frank pleaded, "Jessica, I did not do it. I didn't kidnap anyone. Believe me. Thad can tell you. Thad?"

Thad, eager to vouch for Frank, rattled off, "Frank took the bus, and I almost lost my helicopter when he stole the boat, and we missed school, and we had cookies with Ruth, and

Daddy wasn't home, and they took Gina away in the helicopter, and that's it."

"See. I didn't do it," Frank reiterated.

Jessica, still not wholly convinced, questioned him further. "Then why did you come here?"

Frank leaned in, his voice taking on a hushed urgency. "I know where the ransom money is, Jessica. But I have to explain everything to Mr. Russel. It's the only way I can prove that I'm innocent."

She held up a hand to halt him. "Don't tell me anymore."

Frank paused for a moment, choosing his words carefully. "It's on the island. It's in a compost bin in the shed."

Disbelief shadowed her face. "This is too incredible. How did you get to the island? By helicopter, I suppose?"

"No, by plane," Frank replied.

She scoffed, her patience wearing thin. "Oh, come on. There is no airport there. I can't believe anything you say anymore, Frank. Please?"

As their conversation continued, neither noticed a man stealthily step out onto the balcony from behind the drapes. Thad, oblivious to the tension in the room, began plinking at the piano keys.

Trying to steer the conversation away from the current topic, Frank asked, "How do you like what you're doing now? How do you like the kind of person that you've become? The new Jessica Blair."

With a hint of defensiveness, Jessica responded, "Myron and I sing together, and we work hard together, and I like it a lot."

Frank raised an eyebrow. "You do? You never used to."

She bit her lip, choosing her words carefully. "That never would have worked out between us, and you know it. We were different."

"But you're doing it now. It's the exact same thing," Frank pressed.

Her eyes narrowed, anger simmering. "It's totally different."

Frank's voice rose, frustration evident. "Oh, come on, Jessica. Don't give me that crap. You just didn't want to work for it. You wanted it handed to you. You wanted Prince Charming to come in, sweep you off your feet, and take you under his wing so you could sing your little heart out."

In a swift motion, Jessica's hand connected with Frank's face, delivering a stinging slap. "Take it back. That's not fair."

Jessica's eyes shimmered with anger and sadness, her voice barely above a whisper. "I didn't want to starve waiting for it."

Frank's desperation was palpable. "We can still do it, Jess. We can still be together."

She shook her head, holding back the tears that threatened to spill. "I have to tell you — I should have told you before. Frank —"

He cut her off, his voice filled with pleading. "Let me just say one thing. That's all. Just one more thing: I'll go and won't bother you anymore. I still love you. I mean that. I don't care what happens. I'll always love you, Jess."

At that, Jessica's resolve crumbled, tears streaming down her face as she threw her arms around Frank. "I love you too, but I don't know, Frank. Why did you have to be this way?"

His voice was raw with emotion. "It's the same, Jess. It doesn't matter what you call it. It's the same damn thing. Listen to me."

While they were engrossed in their emotional exchange, Jack Rose stepped in from the balcony, but neither noticed him.

Jessica's voice broke, "Don't say anymore, Frank. I can't any longer. It just won't work out."

His voice trembled, clinging onto the vestiges of hope. "Why? We can have something, Jessica. You know that. If you'd be honest with yourself, you would know there's something here. You know that."

She took a deep breath, the weight of her words settling heavily between them. "It's too late."

Refusing to accept defeat, Frank's voice was urgent. "But what we have is between you and me, and nothing will ever change. It doesn't matter what happens. My feelings aren't going to change. I love you, Jess."

Her following words came as a gut punch. "I'm marrying Myron, Frank."

Suddenly, Frank was released from her embrace, his body moving backward, only to be gripped by the steady hands of Jack Rose. He was too stunned by Jessica's revelation to even notice. As Jack led him to the door, two cops materialized, waiting.

Rose gave a curt command, "Bring the boy."

Thad obediently followed one cop while Frank, Rose, and the other officer exited the suite. Left behind, Jessica stood in the center of the grand room, her sobs echoing through the empty space, a figure of desolation.

12

I nside a dimly lit jail cell, Frank was etching his initials into the grime-coated wall when the metallic groan of the door signaled the guard's entry.

"What are you doing?" the guard demanded, eyeing Frank's impromptu artwork.

Frank shrugged, feigning indifference. "You're treating me like a convict, so I might as well play the part."

With an unamused snort, the guard retorted, "C'mon, let's go. You'll have plenty of time for writing later," and promptly clamped cuffs on Frank's wrists.

As they walked along the corridor, the heavy clink of chains accompanied their footsteps. The cells on either side were filled with the low hum of conversations and disgruntled prisoners. Frank tried to break the tension. "This place is like kindergarten. You enjoy the work here?"

The guard raised an eyebrow. "What do you mean?"

"You like to hear the same story over and over again, you guys."

"Heard 'em all before anyway," the guard replied, uninterested. "They'd probably like you to crack a few jokes for a change." As they approached a door, the guard added, "And hey, no swearing this time. The lieutenant doesn't like that."

Inside the interrogation room, the surroundings were even more chilling. Small, spartan, and sterile, the only break in the monotony was a video camera fixed in a corner. Seated across the table was Detective Sharpe, a solid, middle-aged man with a crewcut that hinted at his no-nonsense demeanor.

"Tell me about the men in the seaplane," Sharpe began without preamble.

"I told you before. I don't know who they were. I couldn't see them," Frank replied, exasperated.

Sharpe continued, relentless in his questioning. "Were they tall or short?"

"I don't know."

"How many did you see?"

"Zero, I saw zero men. That means none. Nothing. No one. Okay?"

Sharpe's face remained impassive. "Where did you pick up the money?"

Frank smirked. "In the boat. You want to know how much horsepower it had?"

The detective shifted tactics. "What made you think Mrs. Russel would pay the ransom?"

"Look," Frank snapped, his patience wearing thin. "I never thought anything. I'm not answering any more questions till I get a lawyer."

Sharpe leaned forward, his voice chilly. "You have one. He's on his way. How long have you known Jessica Blair?"

Frank's response was tinged with defiance. "None of your goddamned business."

For a few moments, the room was steeped in a heavy silence. Finally, Sharpe spoke, each word dripping with menace. "Corbin, you're being charged with kidnapping, grand larceny, hijacking, extortion, crossing a state line with two minors, carrying a dangerous weapon, public mischief... do you want me to go on?"

Unbeknownst to Frank, Detective Jack Rose and Ace Kantor were intently monitoring the questioning in the control booth adjacent to the interrogation room.

"Pretty clever setup," Ace remarked.

Rose responded with a question. "You going to tell him what's involved?"

Ace pondered, "I don't know. If I do, we'll probably never nail the boys inside."

Rose's brows furrowed in concern. "What do you propose to do?"

"I've been thinking about bailing him out. Put him back on the street."

"They'll go for him, you know."

Ace met his gaze, determination shining in his eyes. "Damn right, they will."

Rose hesitated. "And if they kill him?"

"That's the chance that we take."

Rose looked troubled. "Ace? Since when did you start thinking like that?"

Ace replied confidently, "They won't kill him, Rosie. They want the cash too much. He'll lead them to the money and lead us to them."

Sharpe paced around Frank in the interrogation room like a predator circling its prey. "What do you think we should do, Frank?"

With a defiant glint in his eye, Frank replied, "I think you should find the right guy. It's Fox. He's the only one who can verify my story besides the kids."

Sharpe leaned in closer. "Anything else?"

Frank's lips curled into a smirk. "Yeah... play marbles and take a recess."

The Edgewater Hotel stood gracefully by the waterfront, a charming building. A sign painted on one of its walls invitingly read: "FISH FROM YOUR WINDOW." And indeed, that seemed to be the favorite pastime of the residents.

Inside one of the rooms, Fox was reclining, a beer in hand. He dangled a fishing rod out the window, enjoying the simple pleasure of it. Just as he started to reel a fish in, Ace walked in.

"So, what did you find out?" Fox asked without diverting his attention from the catch, unaware of Ace's double role.

"The kid's in town," Ace replied tersely.

Fox's eyes widened slightly, "Well, what are we waiting for?"

"The cops got him," Ace informed him.

Fox looked incredulous, "You got to be kidding? How are we gonna get the money now? That's what I'd like to know. I tell you, man, you really fouled this one up. No kids, no ransom, nothing — We're not even gonna get paid."

By then, Fox had reeled the fish in, revealing it as a baby catfish. "You're still eating," Ace remarked dryly.

Fox scoffed, "Hardly." With that, he tossed it back into the water.

"So, what do you want to do?" Ace queried.

"Get the kid and beat his brains out till he tells us what he did with the dough," Fox declared hotly.

"You can't. I told you. The cops already got him," Ace retorted.

Fox groaned, "I can't believe this happened."

"Well, it did."

Fox's frustration was palpable, "Yeah, well, I ain't sitting around waiting for the sun to shine. We got to do something, and we got to do it now."

"Such as?" Ace prompted.

Fox threw up his hands, "Shit — I don't know." Right then, the phone in the room rang. Both men shot each other a wary glance and lunged for the phone. Ace got to it first.

Meanwhile, two plainclothesmen were getting tickets at the Sea-Tac ticket area in the bustling Seattle/Tacoma International Airport. They escorted young Thad through the crowd.

"We'll get you on the plane, and your mother will meet you back home," one of the plainclothesmen reassured Thad.

Thad's eyes darted anxiously, "But I never saw Daddy, and Gina didn't either."

The man responded soothingly, "You don't worry about your sister. Both of you will be back with your mom before you know it."

Thad's voice wavered, "I'm not worried about her, but I betcha Mommy is."

Traffic controllers monitored the trains in the subway control room on a sophisticated computerized light board. The atmosphere changed abruptly as King dressed sharply in a crisp linen suit, entered. He quietly approached the men from behind and pulled out a gun.

"Good evening, gentlemen," he greeted coolly.

13

———

The plainclothes men and Thad stood patiently at the bustling boarding station, waiting for their train. The place was alive with motion and sound. Amongst the crowd, a serviceman named Earl pushed a vacuum cleaner, appearing to be just another worker. When the subway doors finally slid open, they all stepped in.

Thad eagerly rushed to the front inside the subway car while the plain clothes men took seats nearby. Oblivious to the curious gazes of other passengers, Earl plugged his vacuum cleaner into an outlet, slowly advancing toward the front of the car.

"We are now leaving the south satellite. While the subway is in motion, please stay clear of the doors and hold on to the handrail. Consult the sign above the door for your destination and the direction of the car," a man's voice droned overhead.

One plainclothes man turned to the other, asking, "You been on this before?"

"First time. What about you?"

"Same thing, but my kids told me all about it."

The rhythm of the ride was interrupted when the car unexpectedly halted midway through the tunnel. "Hey, it stopped," Thad noted aloud.

"What's that for?" the first plainclothes man questioned.

"The other train is ahead. It's part of the system," explained the second plainclothes man. But then, darkness swallowed them as the lights flickered out. However, the hum of the vacuum cleaner continued unabated.

"Is that part of the system, too?" the first plainclothes man quipped.

"Must be," his companion responded.

Soon, the subway lurched back into motion, and the lights gradually returned. But, to the plain clothes man's surprise, Thad and Earl had vanished. Panicking, one plain clothes man snatched up the phone, "Hello? Hello?"

Overhead, the same man's voice eerily repeated, "Please remain seated while the subway is in motion."

In the tunnel walkway, Earl led Thad by the hand, hurrying along the edge. They found refuge in an emergency exit just moments before an unlit subway car rushed by, mere inches from them.

Meanwhile, King glanced at a soft beep on his pager in the subway control room. "Ah, time for tea. I'm so sorry you gentlemen won't be able to join me. You will forgive me, won't you?" With a sly smile, he pressed the 'LOCK DOORS' button. The familiar message droned on as the trains sped around the airport perimeter, seemingly mocking the bound and gagged controllers.

Looking gruff and stressed at the opera house dressing room, Myron's business manager barked into the phone, "So where is he? Where the hell is he?"

Jessica, receiving last-minute touches to her dress and makeup, replied with a hint of annoyance, "It's pretty obvious, isn't it? He's not back yet."

"Yeah. Yeah, well, I'm going to give him ten more minutes before I call the whole thing off," the manager snapped.

As dusk settled over the Freeway Park, the occasional passerby strolled along the paths, past tranquil waterfalls and patches of green. Ace sat on a cement block, engrossed in a newspaper. Myron soon arrived, spotted him, and discreetly placed a folded newspaper on a nearby bench. Without a word, he walked away. As multi-colored lights illuminated the park, Ace quickly grabbed the paper. Inside, he found a bounty of cash. His heart raced as he bolted up to the street.

Without missing a beat, Myron climbed into his awaiting limousine, disappearing into the flow of the city's traffic.

The atmosphere in the grand Opera House grew thick with anticipation as the lights dimmed. An excited murmur passed through the audience, and as the curtain slowly rose, Jessica, resplendent in a simple white dress, captured their attention. Her voice, rich and soulful, filled the hall.

"The happiest day of my life," she crooned, every word dripping with emotion.

Meanwhile, backstage in the dressing room, the atmosphere was equally electric, but for different reasons. Myron bustled in, and in the blink of an eye, a swarm of attendants was on him, swiftly changing his attire.

Watching the frenzied activity, the business manager

remarked, "It's about time, Myron. I was about to call Rich Little to come in and take over for you."

Myron grinned, "Thanks, Schmeemo. You're all heart."

"So what happened? Why didn't you call? My blood pressure was up twenty points," the manager continued, clearly irritated.

"Jetfoil broke down. Sorry about your blood pressure. How's the house?"

"SRO. They want to hold you over for a week. I don't know if they feel sorry for you or you're hot, but they're putting their money on the table and not pulling back."

Myron's eyebrows raised in genuine surprise, "What about Vegas?"

"Vegas? Are you kidding? Vegas, Tahoe, Reno, Miami, Chicago, Toronto, and New York, Paris. They want you."

"Really?" Myron inquired, barely able to contain his delight.

"Really, schmeely, would I lie? The calls are like crazy. I can't believe it. Six years you spend out of circulation. Six years, and you're as good as dead, and for six years, we couldn't book you into a garbage can if you'll pardon the expression and look at it now. Same schmucks who had holes in their pockets three months ago are making offers they can hardly afford. We're in business, Myron. And you're number one."

Myron chuckled, "Amazing what good press can do."

"Yeah, that kind of publicity you can't buy. I admire you, you know. If I was you, I couldn't go on. But you can't let these illegal types rule your life. The police will catch up with them. You'll see. You're a mensch."

Myron, clearly touched, managed a simple "Yeah."

Just then, a wave of applause washed over them, making its way backstage. Jessica burst into the dressing room, her eyes sparkling as she threw her arms around Myron. "Myron, you made it. They want you. They're great. They're waiting." The applause was like thunder.

Myron smirked, "How's that for a comeback for an old dog like me?" Without waiting for a response, he strode out, Jessica trailing closely behind, murmuring, "He's a sensation in his old hometown."

The emcee stood confidently back onstage, ready to electrify the already buzzing crowd. "Ladies and gentlemen! Live. Anywhere. For the first time in five years, would you welcome back to beautiful Seattle. Your friend and mine—Ladies and gentlemen, Mr. Myron Russel."

The audience was palpably charged, their gazes riveted on the curtain. As it rose, the stage revealed the most elaborate choreography and set design ever seen in the history of cinema. It was a spectacle so grand, it would've made Busby Berkeley weep. The audience, though too proud to admit it, was awestruck.

Amidst the dizzying display, Myron made his entrance. Weaving through the myriad dancers and props, he finally reached his spot under the spotlight. He took a deep breath with a charming smile directed at his audience. The room grew silent. And then, he began to sing his signature song.

"Welcome back to the good old days," he crooned, voice dripping with emotion. Every audience member hung on to every word, lost in the melody of the old standards.

14

———

At Ivar's Fish Bar, the subtle glow from tiny colored lights shimmered over the dark water. Ferries and sailboats gracefully moved through the sound while a few opportunistic seagulls scavenged for an easy meal. With a fresh-faced appearance from a recently shaved beard, Ace picked up his order of fish and clams and settled at a table across from Jack Rose.

Rose glared at Ace before asking, "What happened?"

"Russel paid us off. He wants us out of it," Ace replied, a hint of annoyance in his voice.

Rose leaned in, his expression earnest. "What about Fox? Does he know yet?"

"No," Ace said, taking a moment to gather his thoughts. "He's waiting for his cut. He's not about to go anywhere. — What about you?"

Rose smirked, "You want the good or bad news?"

"Give me the bad news first. Just don't tell me anything I don't want to hear," Ace grumbled.

"The two local guys who were in training—"

"The ones who took Thad to the airport," Ace interrupted.

"You got it. — They lost him." Rose's words hit Ace like a punch, causing him to knock over his chips in disbelief.

"What?"

"They lost him. An inside job. Pulled him right out of the subway. Our guys didn't even notice."

Ace shook his head, still grappling with the revelation. "You are kidding, I know."

Rose shifted in his seat, sensing the gravity of his next words. "Now. You ready for the good news?"

Ace sighed. "I'm ready for dessert is what I'm ready for."

Rose leaned in closer, "Mrs. Russel got a second ransom demand this morning. The price has doubled."

Ace blinked, stunned. "My father always said I should have studied law. This doesn't make any sense."

"I didn't write the rules," Rose replied, his tone unapologetic.

Ace exhaled deeply, "Thank God. — So, they know about the marked bills, right?"

"They must."

"You're not going to let her deliver the real thing, are you?"

"We sure are. And you and I are picking her up at the airport in fifteen minutes and delivering the whole bundle to the opera house at intermission."

"We what?"

Rose met Ace's incredulous look with a steely one of his own. "Intermission with Mrs. Russel. She wants her kids, and she wants them alive. So, how do we get back in the game and score some points for our side?"

Ace frowned, deep in thought, before suggesting, "I think we throw another fox to the hounds."

"Put some men on Fox?"

"No. Corbin. Back to square one. We put the kid on the street."

·   ·   ·

Meanwhile, at the front desk of the police station, a cop handed Frank his wallet and watch, "Just sign here for your stuff."

Frank's face contorted in confusion, "You mean I'm free? What about the charges? Did they just drop the charges or what?"

The cop, amused by Frank's astonishment, responded, "Let's just say you've got some pretty influential friends working on your side. And they seem to think you're worth a lot."

Frank's face brightened with realization. "Jessica! Jessica and Mr. Russel. I don't believe it." With relief and excitement, he let out a joyful scream, popping some chewing gum into his mouth. "How do I get to the opera house from here?"

"It's five blocks down the street to the monorail. Take that. It'll take you right up behind the center. You can't miss it," the cop replied with a helpful nod.

Frank didn't need to be told twice. He thanked the officer and rushed out the door.

As night blanketed the city, Frank jogged with an elated bounce in his step. However, his happiness was short-lived as a car began trailing him. The vehicle's proximity grew uncomfortably close, sending chills down Frank's spine. Without hesitation, he darted through a narrow alley, leaping over obstacles and desperately trying to escape. But the car was relentless, its horn blaring. Suddenly, a city bus appeared ahead, blocking the car's path. Seizing his chance, Frank sprinted towards the bus and, with adrenaline surging, hopped aboard, leaving his pursuer behind.

Aboard the bus, Frank frantically searched his pockets for change as the vehicle began to move. "Do you have change for a five?" he asked, slightly out of breath. "I know you guys don't like to do this, but it's all I've got right now."

The bus driver glanced at him with a hint of amusement. "No, that's alright. It's free."

Frank blinked in surprise. "What?"

The driver gestured to a sign that read: MAGIC CARPET SERVICE - FREE WHILE YOU SHOP DOWNTOWN.

"I don't know who's crazier. You or me? Thanks," Frank muttered, still trying to process his sudden stroke of luck. He sat, allowing himself a brief moment of reprieve as he looked out the window.

From his vantage point, Frank could see the relentless car that had been tailing him. It blared its horn, swerving aggressively between lanes before finally getting halted by a police officer.

Trying to make light of the situation, Frank called out to the driver, "Crazy drivers in this town, huh?"

The bus driver simply replied, "Not me."

As the bus pulled up to a stop, Frank rushed out and sprinted towards the monorail entrance.

The car that had been trailing him wasn't far behind. It mounted the sidewalk with tires screeching, sending pedestrians scattering in every direction. The door flung open, and Fox emerged, shouting, "Hey, stop him! Stop that guy! Come back here! Hey you!"

Frank's heart raced as he approached the monorail gate. "How much is it?" he asked a girl behind the counter.

"Twenty cents," she replied.

"Do you have change?" But before he could get a response, Fox was upon him.

"Kid, I wanna talk to you," Fox growled.

In a desperate move, Frank shoved a $5.00 bill into the ticket box and darted for the train. Fox refused to pay, deciding instead to leap over the gate in pursuit.

. . .

Frank barely managed to slip inside the train before the doors slid shut, leaving Fox on the platform. Frustrated, Fox ran alongside the train, attempting to pry the doors open and banging on the windows. "What did you do with my money? I want my share. I want my share, you lousy punk!" he yelled, but it was in vain as the train accelerated away.

Frank found an empty seat next to a distinguished bloke in a crisp white suit in the monorail car. Despite his efforts to calm his racing heart, he was on edge. The man with a thick English accent turned to him, "Did you rob a bank?"

Frank, taken aback, stammered, "Huh? Oh, no. He's a friend of mine. Practical joke."

The man chuckled softly, "So was my inquiry. About the bank — a little joke. A conversation starter. Do you live here?"

Frank sighed, "No, I'm sort of on vacation."

The stranger was King, who observed him thoughtfully, "You're very serious for a young man on holiday. Though I suppose all Americans are."

Frank's gaze was pulled back to the window, his attention drifting away from the conversation. King, ever the observer, couldn't help but wonder, "What's caught your attention so?"

15

On the street below the monorail, Fox dashed alongside, a desperate fervor in his eyes, almost reminiscent of a scene from the classic film The French Connection.

In his car, Fox broke every conceivable traffic rule. Running red lights, barreling toward pedestrians, and darting between cars with abandon. His anger evident, he shouted to himself, "When I get you, kid, you're gonna' eat mud."

Back in the monorail, Frank returned his attention to the enigmatic King. "What?" he asked, a little confused.

"Serious," King replied thoughtfully, "Americans strike me as quite serious."

Frank nodded, "They are. And you should be, too. With the way your country is going. I think that's very serious. Just my opinion, though. I don't really know about your queen and all that."

King chuckled, "The king hasn't missed a meal yet."

Frank shot back, "What about the rest of the country?"

"They admire royalty," King said simply.

"That's too bad." Frank mused, his attention again drifting towards the window where he heard the incessant honking of the car below.

King, looking to steer the conversation elsewhere, remarked, "Nice town, Seattle. It's a little like London with all this rain. It's my first time here, and I must say, I quite enjoy it. Are you looking for anyone in particular?"

"No. Just my friend. He's crazy," Frank replied, thinking of Fox.

King leaned back, "Really? There's nothing to see down there. All the real excitement should take place at the opera house. I understand Myron Russel's performance is a killing one."

Frank's ears perked up, "What's that? What about Russel?"

Sensing Frank's heightened interest, King probed further, "I say. Maybe you can help me. I'd like to see Mr. Russel while I'm over, and I understand he's performing at the opera house. Do you know the way?"

"You're heading right for it," Frank said.

"Jolly good," King exclaimed, looking pleased.

Curious, Frank asked, "Say, how long have you been over?"

"Oh, thirty-five years, more or less. A little more than less, actually. But not too much."

"You in town on business?" Frank inquired.

King nodded, "Oh yes. Grave business, I might add."

"Like what?" Frank pressed.

King grinned, "Produce — bananas, artichokes. That sort of thing."

"In Seattle?" Frank raised an eyebrow.

King seemed amused, "Why yes. We're even developing a strain of grape that we can grow in Alaska. The winter wine should be excellent."

Frank chuckled, "You know, you still sound pretty British for thirty-five years."

King smirked, "Well, I should."

Frank looked puzzled, "Why's that?"

King leaned in, "Because it's fake. Can't you tell? Most people can."

Before Frank could respond, the monorail began to pull into the station. "So, where are you from?" Frank asked.

King suddenly shifted to an American dialect, "South Jersey near the swamps. Garden State of the Union. And here's my pal Earl to tell ya' all about it." King's grip tightened on Frank's arm, making any escape impossible.

As the train halted and the port doors opened, a hulking figure, Earl, entered the monorail car. "Earl, tell him about what a nice place is Jersey," King ordered.

Despite the size of the two men, Frank put up a fierce struggle, enough to draw the attention of the monorail staff, who began to gather. The starboard doors soon revealed an irate Fox. He banged the doors, yelling, "Hey, gimme that kid! What are you doing there? I want that kid."

In the brief distraction, Frank managed to wiggle free. King and Earl tried to force their way out as the port doors shut, banging on them. Frank, adrenaline coursing through him and feeling a bit manic, pressed his face against the window, sticking out his tongue and making mocking gestures. The onlookers cheered him on. In all the commotion, the starboard doors reopened, and Fox, now equally exasperated, lunged in.

"What, are you after this kid too?" Fox growled.

But instead of a reply, King and Earl dashed out the door, leaving a frenzied scene behind.

Frank and Fox found themselves in a relentless chase on the bustling station platform, each driven by a different objective. As Frank playfully twisted his ears at Fox, the man's impatience grew, evident by his fervent attempts to break in.

"Come on, kid. Give me a break. You don't need all that dough for yourself," Fox exclaimed in exasperation.

To Frank's surprise, Fox managed to pry the port doors open. The chase resumed as Fox went after him. King and Earl joined in from the other end, effectively boxing Frank in. With the monorail's engines humming to life, both doors slid shut, sealing Frank's perceived fate. But as the monorail began its journey, Frank made a bold move, leaping onto the moving train and scrambling onto its roof.

Fox attempted to follow, but his grip betrayed him, causing him to slip.

Atop the monorail, the rushing scenery below made it impossible for Frank to consider a jump. Desperate, he sprinted towards the train's rear, eyeing a beam from the station roof that appeared tantalizingly close. Frank reached out with every ounce of courage, grasping the shaft just in the nick of time. He used his momentum to swing onto the terminal roof, making his daring escape.

Near the Center House, King and Earl scanned the sea of faces, looking for any sign of Frank. Time was running out, and they weighed their options, eventually abandoning the hunt. However, Fox, driven by relentless determination and greed, persisted. His eyes darted around, scrutinizing fountains and rooftops before he concluded that the building ahead was his best bet.

Inside the Food Circus, a vibrant atmosphere greeted him. The area buzzed with activity with restaurants, exhibits, and even a bandshell. As Fox weaved through the crowd, he glimpsed the majestic rise of the Bubbleator, a domed glass elevator. As its doors hissed open, Frank emerged, trying to blend in. The two adversaries' paths collided unexpectedly.

"Ya' lousy creep," Fox growled.

Reacting swiftly, Frank stomped on Fox's foot and tried to make another getaway. But Fox was nothing if not persistent. Ignoring all caution, he brandished his gun, firing wildly at Frank. Panic ensued. Tables toppled, dinners ruined, and chaos reigned supreme. Yet, the band on stage seemed oblivious, filling the room with the upbeat rhythm of a popular big band number.

In the pandemonium, Fox lost sight of Frank. Frustrated, he snatched a burger from an unsuspecting diner and took a bite, only to spit it out in disgust when he realized it was cold. He knew he had lost Frank for now, but the chase was far from over.

16

Outside the opera house, an unmarked car flanked by a police escort came to a halt. Emerging from the vehicle were Pamela, Ace, and Rose. As they ascended the steps, Rose clutched an attaché case.

In the bustling lobby of the concert hall, the hum of chatter and rustle of programs filled the air. Amid the concertgoers, Pam, Ace, and Rose approached an usher, who promptly guided them toward the elevator. They stepped inside and selected the floor for the balcony.

Upon reaching the lower balcony, the subtle notes of instruments tuning could be heard in the distance. The usher guided the trio further, leading them to Loge Two, a box near the stage. Rose carefully placed the case on the seat, opening it to reveal its contents: stacks upon stacks of money.

"Well, that's it. All we have to do now is wait," Rose remarked as they closed the door behind them and moved to another box.

Elsewhere, just two loge boxes over, King discreetly entered Loge Six and settled into his seat.

Navigating through the elegant hallways lined with concertgoers, Ace cautioned the usher, "Just keep your eyes open if anyone comes by. But I don't want you sitting right on the door, okay?" The usher simply nodded in understanding.

Pam, Ace, and Rose finally settled into Loge One. They took their seats just as the ambient light began to soften and the expectant murmur of the audience quieted.

Somewhere distant, in an underground garage, a white limousine smoothly transitioned off a ramp. It stationed itself near the service area, its headlights fading into darkness. Inside, Thad and Gina, their mouths gagged, had their eyes fixed on a TV screen showing an episode of "*Batman.*" A soft 'beep' from a pager broke the silence.

In response, King in Loge Six silenced his device and sent a signal back.

The curtains gracefully ascended on stage to reveal Myron seated before a grand piano. A wave of applause washed over the hall as he started his soulful solo.

Detective Jack Rose, Pamela Russel, and undercover agent Ace Kantor sat intently, their eyes scanning the opposite loge for any signs of activity. But Loge Two remained eerily still.

Outside in the hall, the anxious usher fidgeted, taking drags from his cigarette one after another.

The service elevator door slid open elsewhere to reveal Earl and the kids. They transitioned onto a battery-powered mini-cart and began their journey. They sped past the scenery shop, maneuvered around flats, lumber, and sets under construction, then took a series of ramps upwards. The mini-cart journey ended, and they continued on foot down a dimly lit hallway, making their way to an exit.

· · ·

Upon reaching the upper balcony hallway, Earl opened the door, guiding the kids to their section. The area was sparsely populated, the majority of the audience already engrossed in the concert below.

On the upper balcony, the kids sat at the top, offering them an almost bird's eye view of the stage below. Earl retreated to leave them alone after ensuring their gags were firmly in place. Despite their constrained situation, the kids' attention was drawn irresistibly to the stage, where they could spot their father performing.

Myron's fingers gracefully danced on the piano keys on the stage, evoking a heartwarming melody. But it wasn't just him; a spotlight revealed Jessica, poised to add her voice to the performance.

At the stage door, chaos seemed to brew. Frank, evidently out of breath, barreled into the backstage area, causing a stir among the crew. A particularly burly stagehand confronted him with a skeptical gaze.

"I've got to talk to Jessica Blair. It's important," Frank pleaded.

The sturdy man raised an eyebrow, not budging. "Sorry, you can't. She's on."

"You've got to stop her. They're after her, too. They're going to kill her. I have to warn her," Frank's voice grew more frantic.

"What are you talking about? Who are you, anyway?" the stagehand demanded, suspicion evident in his voice.

From a distance, the call for silence rang out. The stage manager, visibly agitated, whispered a command to his assistant. "Find out what all that commotion is back there. And whatever it is, get rid of it."

As the assistant approached, his intention clear, he said, "All right, buddy, let's go. You've got to pay for your ticket just like the rest of them. Now move."

"But I've got to see Jessica," Frank protested.

"Sure you do. Give me a hand with this clown, will ya?" With those words, the assistant and two other stagehands lifted Frank off the ground.

"You can't do this. You don't know what you're doing. Stop," Frank shouted.

The ruckus had drawn more attention. With impeccable timing, Fox burst into the area, a predatory glint in his eyes. "Aha! So they got you, huh?" Without hesitation, he lunged at Frank's throat. The sheer urgency of the situation seemed to amplify Frank's strength. Frank scrambled up a ladder, breaking free from his captors, with Fox in hot pursuit. A brutal struggle ensued, with Fox trying to wrench Frank's feet off the bars and Frank, in desperation, stomping Fox's hands with such force that the sound of bones crunching echoed in the area.

Frantic, Frank raced along a catwalk, the looming shadow of his pursuers close behind him. Each door he came across seemed to be against him—locked or immovable. However, luck was finally on his side when he found an unlocked door, which he quickly entered and locked behind him.

One of the stagehands, in frustration, said, "I'll get a key." But Fox, always prepared, revealed a set of burglar's picks from his jacket. With practiced ease, he began to work on the lock.

High above the stage, Frank tried desperately to get Jessica's attention in the lighting bank, leaning precariously over the edge and shouting her name. On stage, despite her magnificent performance, Jessica felt a disturbance. She glanced around, trying to locate the source of her unease. Yet the blinding stage lights made her unable to discern anything unusual.

On the lighting bank, Frank's anxiety had him stomping his foot in frustration. No one below could hear or see him amidst the dazzling lights and rich music.

Elsewhere, in Loge Six, King, ever the master of deceit, fumbled with a contact lens case, letting one of the lenses drop. "Pardon me, I'm frightfully sorry," he leaned over and politely told the couple next to him. "But I think I just lost one of my contact lenses."

The couple began to rise, probably out of courtesy or concern, but King quickly stopped them. "Please, don't move. You're quite liable to step on it." Using this ruse as a cover, King slowly and methodically began his crawl from loge six to loge four and finally to loge two. Along the way, he exchanged pleasantries with another theatergoer. "Contact lens. Miserable little devils, aren't they?" he remarked with a smile, ensuring he didn't draw any unnecessary suspicion.

Meanwhile, Earl was on a mission of his own. He skillfully maneuvered a vehicle through the scenery shop. He sped down a corridor, stopping decisively at the door with a foreboding sign: DANGER! KEEP OUT. HIGH VOLTAGE. Earl, unfazed, entered the electrical room without hesitation. Once inside, he approached the main breaker, pausing momentarily to check the time.

.   .   .

Back on the catwalk, two stagehands, one of whom was the manager's assistant, scrambled to find the right key for the locked door, their bunch of keys jingling noisily. Not too far away, at another door, Fox appeared equally vexed. Having failed with one lock pick, he scratched his head in puzzlement and tried another.

Back on the lighting bank, Frank felt cornered. As he heard the rattling of the locks attempting to open the doors leading to him, he inched toward the center of the bank. From this vantage point, his eyes darted below, trying to make sense of the unfolding drama.

Suddenly, Frank's attention was seized by a familiar figure in a white suit in Loge Two. There was King, discreetly pilfering the money-laden attaché case. Frank watched, horrified, as King began his careful retreat.

King saw him and mouthed, "Ta-ta."

Amidst this tension, the song down on the stage ended gracefully. The audience applauded, oblivious to the high-stakes game above and around them. Frank's desperation grew, realizing the futility of his position.

"There he is! That's him!" Frank shouted, his voice barely audible amidst the clapping and cheering.

Desperate, Frank made one last plea. "Jessica? Jessica?" But the crowd's noise drowned out his voice, rendering his efforts to warn her in vain.

17

———

In Loge One, Pam, Ace, and Rose joined the theater's applause, their emotions on a knife's edge. Though their attention was mainly on the stage, they occasionally glanced at Loge Two, scanning for any signs of movement.

Down on stage, Myron and Jessica, still reveling in the success of their performance, took their bows hand-in-hand. The audience's response was deafening, like the rolling sounds of a storm. The curtain fell, only to rise again to the shouts for an encore. The two performers took one final, deep bow and gracefully exited, with the curtain once again falling behind them.

The calm on stage was in stark contrast to the chaos unfolding above. On the lighting bank, Fox and his entourage of stagehands made their entry, their sights set on Frank. But Frank wasn't one to be cornered easily.

"Let me go," he pleaded, his voice shrill with panic. He

spotted King with the money. "He's getting away. He's got the money. Would you get off of me?"

A scuffle ensued, fists flew, and grunts of exertion filled the air. Frank broke free with a surge of adrenaline, only to be tackled by Fox. As he was pushed toward the edge, Fox hissed, "I want my dough, punk."

Suddenly, Frank found himself dangling precariously from the lighting batten. The intense heat seared his palms. "Help me, Fox," he cried out, desperation evident.

Fox's only response was a demand for the whereabouts of the stolen loot. He brutally pushed away the stagehands, attempting to help. Losing his grip, Frank's voice rose to a scream, echoing through the theater.

From the upper balcony, Thad and Gina, finally free of their gags, caught sight of the horrifying scene below. "Hey, look, Gina," Thad shouted. "It's Frank! Daddy, Daddy! There's Frank!"

In Loge One, panic gripped Pam. "That was my son," she exclaimed. "They're here!"

Back on the lighting bank, Frank clung to the batten, which was now nearly too hot to touch. As his strength waned, a sturdy man tried to intervene. "Come on, let me in there. You just hang on, son. I'll get you out."

But time was running out. Frank's voice, quivering with pain and fear, echoed throughout the theater. "Hurry. I can't—"

Suddenly, darkness enveloped the theater as Earl pulled down the handle of the main breaker box. The blackout was punctuated by the piercing screams of the audience and the thunderous sound of the curtain tearing.

In the black void, the stage manager's voice commanded, "Get those backup lights on!" A faint voice, filled with anguish, reached out from the depths of the darkness.

"He got the money," Frank's voice echoed, filled with pain and determination. "I saw him. Right up there. He's got it all."

A devastated scene revealed itself as the backup generator lights flickered back on. Stagehands hurriedly tried to clear the wreckage. The curtain lay torn, and Frank lay sprawled, battered but still conscious amidst its tatters on stage.

"Right up there," he whispered again, his voice a mere shadow of its former self.

In the opulent hallway of the loge, two ushers briskly approached Ace and Rose.

"You two," Ace commanded, "Get your men. Block every exit. Jack, you come with me." Without hesitation, the group rushed to the far side.

The atmosphere tensed immediately after bursting into Loge Two: the money was gone. Whipping around to address the usher, Ace demanded, "You here the whole time?"

"Sure was," the usher replied, seemingly unruffled.

"Nobody went in?" Ace's tone was incredulous.

"No, sir."

Meanwhile, the service elevator door slid open, revealing King's hands gripping the attaché. With a swift move, he climbed aboard the mini-cart, which Earl steered through a hallway and out a door. Upon reaching the service area, they abandoned their ride, instead opting for the waiting limo. The vehicle effortlessly moved through the garage doors, sped up a ramp, and continued toward a brilliantly illuminated fountain. Not far from the water feature, a helicopter awaited. Intensely driven by their mission, King and Earl transferred to the chopper and were soon enveloped by the night sky.

Thad and Gina eagerly pressed the button to descend inside the grand house's elevator. Up on the upper balcony, Pamela frantically searched for her children. Her voice, tinged with worry, pierced through the hushed atmosphere, "Thad? Gina? Where are you?"

Frank was battling his dizziness back on the stage, trying to get back on his feet after the unexpected fall. Off to the side, the stage manager was barking orders. "Come on. Get that curtain off him. Move." As the curtain started its ascent, Frank, a bit thrashed, managed to extricate himself. Still, in their seats, the audience watched with bated breath as he tried to recover his composure.

"Sorry," he began hesitantly, "Is there anyone out there?" Blinded by the stage lights, he glared at the wings where Fox and the stagehands looked, ready to attack. The technicians, for the moment, held them back.

"Okay. Get the curtain back down," the stage manager's voice held a note of exasperation.

"It's stuck," came the technician's frustrated reply.

Caught in the spotlight, Frank addressed the audience again, "Sorry, I don't... I don't really... don't usually drop in like this." He could feel the crowd's restlessness and tried to salvage the situation. "If I knew I was going to be here, I would have been ready for it. What the hell am I doing here?"

As the reality of the situation began to dawn on him, Frank's nervousness grew palpable. Sweat beaded his forehead. His adversaries, waiting in the wings, kept his anxiety levels high.

"They were uhh... pretty... pretty good," he attempted, only to be met with a smattering of applause.

"You know, I've never been in a hall this size before, and I... don't... hardly know what to do. Actually, I'm so tired I don't even know what I'm saying anymore."

From the crowd, a voice called out cheekily, "Then at least say something funny."

Laughter rippled through the audience, breaking the tension, if only for a moment.

In the wings of the grand stage, a technician fiddled with a circuit, his brow furrowed in concentration. The stage manager, a tall figure with a natural aura of authority, hovered nearby, watching the technician's every move.

"Get it yet?" the stage manager inquired impatiently.

The technician shook his head, signaling that the circuit wasn't functioning yet. Amidst this tension, an usher sidled up to the stage manager, whispering hurriedly, "Let the kid stay on. Give him a little music. The doors are locked. The police are checking the house. They need some time."

Nodding, the stage manager signaled the conductor, and with a flick of the baton, the orchestra started playing an intro.

On stage, amidst the grandeur and the spotlight, Frank glanced around, confused but trying to go with the flow. He took a gracious bow, "Thank you. See ya." However, as he attempted to exit, the manager's assistant, a spry young woman, nudged him back onto the stage.

"Just keep doing what you're doing, and don't stop. You're great," she whispered hurriedly.

18

Thrown back into the spotlight, Frank blinked in confusion as the orchestra played the cue several times. As he began to grasp the situation, he tried to charm the audience, "Hi. My name is Frank Corbin, and I'm a songwriter by day and a bus driver by night. — In my real life, that is. Sorry, it's the other way around."

His humor earned a smattering of chuckles from the crowd. With newfound confidence, he continued, "You know, a funny thing happened to me on the way to work yesterday morning. I was driving my bus, minding my own business, keeping an eye out for radar, and stopping at all the right railway tracks when this porky guy in a yellow mask suddenly put a gun to my head." The audience roared with laughter at his anecdote. "And he says, 'Keep your hands on the wheel and your eyes on the road, kiddo, or I'll blow your brains out right through your exhaust manifold.'" The audience breaks up. "This is a hijacking. Remember Chowchilla? Well, so did this guy. And he even came out for the show. Let's bring him on."

Gesturing at Fox with a nod, Frank tried to bring him onto

the stage, but Fox, not wanting any part of it, darted away. "He's a little shy right now. Well, that's one way to get rid of your friends," Frank quipped, earning more laughs.

His demeanor shifted to sincerity as he addressed the weary audience, "Anyway, it's late. And you probably haven't slept for two days. I know I haven't. So, before you go, I'd like to do something for you for being such a great audience. I mean, they're going to lock me up when I finish here, and I just don't want you to go home mad. I just want you to go home." Drawing another round of laughter, Frank approached the piano, striking the first notes of his best song.

"I always wanted to do this one as a duet, but it's not easy when you've only got two hands." Frank began to sing. "I love you so very much, and you will never know why. You mean so much to me that sometimes I must cry." He's improved. A lot. It's because he's so nervous. "My star is with me wherever I go, always in the sky, even when you don't show."

As he sang, his voice gaining strength and confidence, Thad and Gina moved closer to him, leaning on the piano, sharing smiles.

In the audience, a well-dressed man named Danny Fast, a music promoter, listened intently to Frank's performance. Beside him, his girlfriend looked equally intrigued. As Frank's song wrapped up, she leaned over and kissed Danny's cheek.

"Very nice. Very nice," Danny murmured appreciatively. "A little rough but very nice."

"You like it, Danny?" his girlfriend asked with a smile.

"Yeah," he responded, his eyes still on the stage. "Nice bit with the kids. Cute. Real cute. I like that."

· · ·

Ace, the cop, gently tapped the stage manager on the shoulder in the dimly lit wings. "We're all through," he stated confidently. The stage manager, in turn, signaled to a technician who promptly pressed a button, setting a series of events into motion.

On stage, as the curtain began its descent, Frank's melodic voice filled the theater, his gaze fixed on the slowly closing curtain. He hesitated momentarily, then said, "Have you ever felt that you've been someplace before?" But before continuing, he cut himself short and started singing again, "So, this love's for you, cause this love's for you. This love's for you. — Thank you. Thank you very much. I guess?"

The audience erupted in applause, cheering wildly as Frank took a bow. As the curtain completed its descent, the stage filled with people. Thad and Gina, two enthusiastic fans, embraced Frank. But their reunion was interrupted by a frantic voice calling out, "Thad? Gina?"

"It's Mommy. Gina, it's Mommy," Thad exclaimed as they spotted their Mom.

Suddenly, with a devious grin, Fox collared Frank, grappling him to the ground, almost choking him. "All right. Cough it up, Franco. You ain't no hit with me," he growled.

Pamela burst onto the stage and hugged both Thad and Gina. The reunion was heartfelt but quickly overshadowed by Fox's aggression. Frank watched from the sidelines, his expression softening.

"Don't you ever give up, slob?" Frank retorted, struggling for breath.

Thad moved to kick Fox, but Pamela stopped him. "He's hurting Frank, Mom," Thad said.

"I want my share, Franco. I want what's coming to me," Fox insisted.

Before things could escalate further, Ace stepped in, lifting Fox off Frank. Rose stood behind him, backed by cops. "That's enough, Fox. Let's go."

"What? You turn into some freakin' crewcut? What's with you?" Fox exclaimed.

"You're under arrest, Fox. Take him," Rose commanded, and the cops hauled Fox away.

"Hey, all I wanted is my fair share," Fox called out.

"You'll get your share," Ace shot back.

"So, what are you doing this for? I thought you were my partner. I didn't do nothing. You know that. It was Russel. Russel hired me," Fox argued.

"Really? Why you?"

"Pay off gambling debts," Fox stated.

"And the other guys?"

"Insurance policy, I guess," Fox said.

"That's all I wanted to hear, Fox. You know what you're going to be charged with? Kidnapping, grand larceny, hijacking, extortion, crossing a state line with two minors, carrying a dangerous weapon, public mischief... should I go on?"

"What about child endangerment?" Fox smirked.

"Child endangerment." Ace retorted.

"I could be an informant?" Fox offered as a last-ditch effort.

Frank studied Ace's face. "Weren't you one of—Weren't you with him in the boat? Monterey?"

"That's right," Ace said.

"Well, who are you? Really?" Frank asked. In response, Ace showed him his police badge.

The stage manager cut in. "Come on, everybody. Let's go."

Just then, Danny Fast pushed his way through the crowd and pumped Frank's hand. "Terrific stuff. Caught your act. Loved it. You represented?"

"No, but I think I could use a lawyer right now," Frank replied.

"Dynamite. That's not exactly what I do. Someplace we can talk?" Danny stuffed a business card into Frank's palm.

"Lieutenant, I hope you're not letting him just walk out of here. This man is a criminal," Pamela interjected.

"Mrs. Russel, he's not a criminal," Rose clarified.

"He's not an animal, Mom. He's Frank. Fox is the animal," Thad defended.

"Yeah, and we had fun with Frank," Gina added.

The stage manager raised his voice again, ushering people off the stage. "Would everyone please leave the stage? Clear the stage now."

Pamela remained insistent. "I insist that you take him into custody. It's the very least you could do."

Ace pulled Frank aside. "Listen, Frank. There's no charges. You're free to go. Now get out of here and stay out of trouble, okay."

Frank hugged Thad and Gina. They waved goodbye and smiled while Pamela frowned. Frank left, and Danny went with him.

"Listen, Frank, I'll tell you what I can do for you. My name's Danny. I'm a people manager. A&R. Talent Scout. I've moved a lot of artists to the top, fast, and you're going to be my next project. All right?" Danny said.

Ace whispered to Rose, "Stay with him, Rosie." Rose and a couple of cops followed Frank out.

Pamela huddled with her children and showered them with kisses. "Are you both all right? I missed you so much," she said, her voice breaking.

"Frank didn't do it, Mommy. It was Fox. He had a mask, and he looked mean, and he smelled funny," Thad said.

"Are you going to be away again when we go home, Mom?" Gina asked.

"Never for very long, Gina. I promise," Pamela assured them.

"It was a biiiiiggg blaaaack guuun, Mom," Thad continued.

Pamela hugged her children tightly. "I love you both so much, you know. We'll go away together. I promise."

"We love you too, Mom, but you're never at home, and we don't want to go anywhere now. We just want to be with you, okay?" Gina said.

"I promise I'll stay with you, baby," Pamela reassured.

"Cross your heart and hope to die?" Gina asked.

"Yes," Pamela said. "Double promise. Cross my heart."

Gina turned to Thad. "You think we can trust her this time?"

Thad winked back at Gina, and they both hugged their Mom, believing in the promises she'd just made.

A soft glow illuminated the front of the island house as the door creaked open, revealing Myron and Ruth. Myron squinted into the darkness, trying to find his bearings.

"Don't bother, Ruth. I can find my way, all right. You just go back to bed and try to get some sleep," Myron advised.

"But Mr. Russel, two other men were looking for you after your children left," Ruth said, her voice laced with worry.

"Good night, Ruth," Myron responded, brushing off her concern.

"You're not in any trouble, I hope?" Ruth asked, her eyes searching Myron's face for an answer.

Myron paused. His expression was contemplative. "Ruth, I grew up with trouble and never thought it would leave. But I've finally reached the age where all that is behind me." With those parting words, he disappeared into the shadows.

As he approached the gardener's shed, he flicked on his flashlight, its beam scanning the area. It settled on a compost bin. Carefully, he opened it, dug inside, and retrieved a pack. Upon flipping it open, his eyes lit up as they fell upon a substantial amount of money. He tenderly caressed it, murmuring, "Ah, Jessica, my girl. You're all right."

The gentle sound of water splashing caught his attention as dawn broke. Myron, now standing on a dock shrouded in mist, pocketed a gun and ensured the money pack was safely secured. Signs around the property warned: PRIVATE KEEP OUT! As the jetfoil neared the dock, bumping lightly against it, Myron boarded with the assistance of a crew member.

Inside the passenger cabin, Myron received a polite greeting from a purser. "Foggy morning, isn't it, sir?"

"Never seen better," Myron responded with a satisfied smile.

A woman seated nearby nudged her husband, her voice a whisper. "I think that's that famous singer. Must be pretty important for us to stop like that. Do you know who I mean?" But the old man, equipped with a hearing aid, simply looked around, clearly uninterested.

Upon entering the pilothouse, Myron was met with familiar faces. The purser offered to take his bag, but he declined.

The captain, seated at the helm, turned to greet him. "Well, Myron, how are you keeping yourself?"

"Top shape. As usual," Myron replied with confidence.

"I hear you were sold out last night. I'm sorry I missed it," the captain said, genuinely regretful.

"We broke house records," Myron said with a hint of pride.

The captain smiled warmly. "Well, you certainly deserve it after all these years."

"And this is just the beginning," Myron proclaimed, his voice filled with determination. "The new Myron Russel is going to sweep the nation."

The captain raised an eyebrow, his interest piqued. "Good for you. And you'll be a better man for it, right?"

Myron smirked, leaning back casually. "You said it. Not me." After a beat, he added, "Do you have any coffee?"

19

The monorail rushed by, its sleek form blurring into the city's skyline. Church bells echoed through the streets, announcing the arrival of a sleepy Sunday morning in the heart of town.

Jessica stood elegantly in front of a mirror inside the plush Crown Suite of The Seattle Plaza Hotel. She had been awake for hours, and now an attendant worked diligently to perfect her wedding dress.

"It should come up just a little bit more, I think. Yes, like that," Jessica directed, her fingers tracing the fabric.

Her gaze wandered around the suite, brimming with colorful flowers and wrapped presents. She turned back to the attendant, a question in her eyes. "Did you check with the desk to see if there were more flowers?"

"Not yet, Miss," the attendant replied, focusing on the delicate task.

Jessica's face creased with a hint of worry. "What about my mother? Has she come in yet?"

"Her plane isn't due till eleven o'clock, I believe. The driver will pick her up at the airport."

Jessica sighed, the reality of the day washing over her. "Ohhh, I can't believe this is really happening to me. It's like a dream."

The attendant smiled politely. "If you say so, Miss."

As Jessica's eyes scanned the room again, she murmured, "I hope I haven't forgotten anything. Have you checked the mail yet? There might be more presents."

"I will if you like," the attendant offered.

"No, no. Don't bother. I'll do it. I need the exercise. I'm getting so fat," Jessica said with a playful pout. Of course, she wasn't overweight, but many brides-to-be shared similar sentiments.

The young bride moved closer to the door. "Small weddings are so much nicer than big, ghastly affairs, don't you think?"

The attendant agreed, "Absolutely."

As Jessica reached for the door handle, she was surprised. Her old friend Frank lay there, sound asleep in the hallway, curled up outside her suite. Gently, she nudged him awake.

"Frank? Frank, what are you doing here?" she exclaimed.

He looked up, his eyes glassy. "You can't do it, Jessica. You can't."

"I can't do what? What are you talking about? You can't stay here. My mother's coming, and Myron will be back soon, and you—" She was cut off as a disheveled Frank stumbled into the suite. The attendant looked on, her eyes wide.

"Can I get you some coffee?" she inquired politely. Frank simply smiled in response.

Jessica, her patience waning, confronted him. "Frank, why do you have to do these crazy things? I don't understand. You make it very hard for me, you know."

"No. I don't," he murmured.

Exasperated, she said, "The last thing I need is for you, Mr. Jinx, to hang around on my wedding day, Frank."

Frank's eyes grew intense. "He's a fraud."

She frowned, "What?"

"Myron's a fraud."

Jessica's voice grew sharp. "You are insulting my fiancé, I'll have you know, and I don't like it one bit. Frank, if it's any of your business, which it isn't. He loves me, and I love him, and that's all that matters right now. Thank you."

But Frank persisted, "He's too old for you."

Jessica retorted, "And you're too young."

His voice rising, Frank demanded, "Where is he, Jessica?"

She looked away, her tone cold. "Wouldn't you like to know?" But as he grabbed her arm, she gasped, "I bet you would."

As the attendant returned with the coffee, Frank's grip loosened. He took the cup and sipped slowly, deliberately ignoring Jessica.

After a moment, she relented, "He went to the island."

Frank's eyebrows shot up. "What for?"

She hesitated, then said, "I told him what you told me. About the money. He's getting it now so he can return it to Pamela."

Without hesitation, Frank snatched the phone and began to dial frantically.

Jessica eyed him warily. "Who are you calling?"

With a smirk, Frank echoed her earlier words, "Wouldn't you like to know?"

In a dimly lit office at the police station, Ace and Rose stood, intensely studying a flowchart. Despite their efforts, many of the boxes remained empty.

Rose frowned, tracing a line with his finger. "Well, it's obvious that he's working for these people out of Canada. I just don't see where he fits."

Just as Ace was about to respond, the sharp ring of the

phone pierced the silence. He swiftly picked it up, answering with a curt, "Kantor." After several brief acknowledgments, he abruptly hung up and turned to Rose with urgency in his eyes.

"Let's go. I want you to contact the Coast Guard and Canadian Customs. Get dispatch on the phone. We got to stop Russel before he crosses that border."

They didn't waste another second, purposely rushing out of the office.

Meanwhile, in the luxurious ambiance of the Crown Suite, Frank replaced the phone's receiver, his expression unreadable.

Curious and slightly concerned, Jessica asked, "Who did you call, Frank?"

He met her gaze with a finality that made her heart drop. "He's not gonna show."

Confused, she pressed, "What are you talking about?"

"No wedding today," he responded bluntly. "Thank you." And without further warning, he took her hand, pulling her out of the room.

Across the border, the grandeur of the Conservatory at the Empress Hotel echoed with the soft rustling of foreign newspapers. Basil, immaculately dressed, flipped through them with practiced ease. The heavy wooden door opened to admit King and Earl, who placed an attaché case on the table before him.

"You have been tardy, gentlemen. I've been expecting you since five o'clock this morning," Basil remarked, smoothly opening the case. The sight of the money inside caught his attention, and he examined it meticulously - smelling it, holding it to the light, and finally setting one bundle aside. With a wicked grin, he emptied the contents of his pipe onto the stack, setting it aflame.

"I'm sorry I have to do this to you, gentlemen. But you see, the money is no good," Basil began as the two men stared in horror. "It's counterfeit, and it's not even a worthy copy. It has police written all over it, unfortunately."

He presented a bill to a distraught-looking Earl whose eyes welled up. "So, all that leaves, of course, is the original sum. And I am disappointed that you hadn't thought of it sooner. Much sooner," Basil finished, his smile colder than ever.

Onboard the Jetfoil, the gentle hum of the vessel's machinery filled the pilothouse. Myron, restless, glanced over at his case by the door. Beside him, the captain and copilot were engrossed in monitoring various readouts.

"How much farther?" Myron asked impatiently.

Without taking his eyes off the controls, the captain replied, "Forty-five minutes."

The copilot interjected, "Chop is up to seven now."

"We'll take her up a few feet," decided the captain.

As the Jetfoil adjusted its altitude, rising slightly so that only its jets touched the water, an unexpected sight came into view. A State Police seaplane was drawing near, flying alongside them.

20

Inside the well-lit pilothouse of the jetfoil, the men exchanged glances as they peered out the window.

"Looks like company," the co-pilot remarked, an eyebrow raised. Beside him, Myron shifted uncomfortably.

"Probably going to give you a speeding ticket," Myron quipped, trying to ease his tension.

The captain chuckled, "Yeah. We're breaking all the records."

Suddenly, the radio crackled to life, drawing their attention. "This is the Washington State Police to the Flying Princess Two. Over," a voice reported.

Gripping the microphone, the captain responded, "Flying Princess Two to State Police. We read you. Over."

"Flying Princess," the voice continued, "you've got a fog problem and heavy tanker traffic ten minutes south of Victoria in the Juan de Fuca Strait. Washington State Ferry control requests that you return to your home base. You cannot dock in Victoria at this time. Over."

"Roger. We copy," the captain acknowledged, signing off. He

leaned back in his chair with a frustrated sigh. "Well, ain't that a sonofabitch."

The co-pilot, peering at the radar, remarked, "Looks clear on the radar."

The captain mused, "Maybe an oil spill or something. They always have these damn accidents out here."

"We don't want to be involved in any accidents now, do we?" Myron interjected.

The captain nodded. "You said it."

"You want to flip to see who tells them?" the co-pilot suggested, pointing aft and revealing a glinting silver dollar.

"Just call it in the air, Stan," the captain retorted.

But Myron's voice sliced through their banter, "Maybe there's no need to tell them. We'll just keep heading straight up like nothing happened." As the words left his mouth, he produced a gun, leveling it at the two men.

The co-pilot began, "What the—"

The captain, swallowing hard and feeling the weight of the moment, said, "Yeah, I guess we will. Save your money, Baker. Looks like we're going to Victoria."

Meanwhile, high above Puget Sound, the humming of a Seattle Police seaplane's engine was evident as it swept gracefully over a cluster of sailboats, setting its sights north.

Ace sat rigidly beside the pilot inside the seaplane, his gaze fixed ahead. "They're just up ahead," the pilot informed. "How do you want to come in?"

"Just slow and easy," Ace replied, "right from behind."

By the serene island boathouse, the sound of an approaching jet boat disrupted the morning calm. Frank, with the throttle wide open, expertly maneuvered the boat to dock. Beside him sat Jessica, her wedding dress billowing gently in the sea breeze, an odd juxtaposition to their current setting.

Busy with her chores, Ruth paused to hose down the dock, glancing up at their arrival. "Ah, you're returning the boat. And you brought Jessica with you. How nice," Ruth remarked, a hint of surprise in her tone.

Frank, with a hint of urgency, asked, "Where's Myron?"

"He went to Victoria," Ruth replied, wiping her hands on a cloth.

"When?" Frank pressed.

"He just left on the hydrofoil not more than an hour or so. Can I get you kids some breakfast?"

Turning briefly to Jessica, Frank muttered, "What did I tell you?"

Ignoring him, Ruth greeted Jessica warmly, "Hello there, Jessica. Nice to see you again. And how are the singing lessons coming along?"

But before she could get a response, Frank had already started the jet boat, propelling them away from the boathouse.

On the jet boat, the engine's roar made conversation challenging. Jessica, visibly upset, refused to meet Frank's gaze. "You're making a big mistake, Frank," she protested.

Frank retorted, "No, I'm not. I'm keeping you from making an even bigger one."

Jessica's voice dripped with sarcasm, "Oh, every girl should have a friend as kind and thoughtful as you are."

"You're damn right," Frank snapped back, gunning the boat's engine harder. The boat sliced through the water, leaving everything else in its wake. The knot meter flashed 52 KPH. The cold wind had Jessica shivering.

"This is stupid, Frank. I want you to take me back," she shouted over the engine's roar.

"You want to see Myron, don't you?" Frank replied a hint of challenge in his eyes.

"Of course I do," Jessica admitted.

Frank grinned, "Okay. Then, just hang on tight."

Meanwhile, the sleek Flying Princess jetfoil danced upon the waves, its wake creating ripples that shimmered in the morning light. Above, the State Police seaplane circled like a hawk, monitoring its every move.

Inside the passenger cabin of the jetfoil, three women were engrossed in filling out survey reports. "What did you put for the ride, Maryann?" one asked.

"Smooth. Much smoother than I expected," Maryann replied.

"And noise level?" the first woman pressed.

"It's not bad at all," Maryann responded.

A third woman said, "I think they should continue the service. It's so much faster than the Princess Marguerite."

"You can say that again. That tug is for the birds," the first woman agreed.

The third woman chuckled, "Still, my only complaint is that there's no room for my Fiat."

Her two friends exchanged amused glances, shaking their heads in mock exasperation.

Inside the pilothouse, tension filled the air. The captain, gripping the controls, tried to reason with the man beside him. "This is crazy, Myron. Are you sure you're feeling all right?" There was no response. Myron's face was unreadable, but the gun he pressed into the captain's ribs spoke volumes.

"What's gotten into you? Do you realize what you're doing?" the captain continued, desperation creeping into his voice.

Myron's gaze remained steely. "I know exactly what I'm doing. I'm going to Victoria, and you're coming with me. We'll arrive on time, just like it says in the schedule. You wouldn't want them to cancel the service now, would you?"

Just then, the radio buzzed to life. A voice, thick with authority, came through: "State Police to Flying Princess Two. You have heavy water and air traffic ahead. Will you return to Seattle? Do you copy? Over."

The captain instinctively reached for the microphone, but Myron's warning stopped him cold. "Don't answer it."

The voice persisted, "Flying Princess. We know you can read us. Please acknowledge. Over."

"Shut it off," Myron ordered tersely. The captain complied.

A Coast Guard jet helicopter loomed somewhere above the Juan de Fuca Strait, heading north. Inside, Jack Rose exchanged a look with the radioman. The latter broadcasted, "Attention all cruisers near Port Angeles and Port Townsend. We have a runaway jetfoil in the Juan de Fuca Strait traveling north by northwest, about twenty-five minutes this side of Victoria. Please proceed to intercept the vessel before she crosses into Canada."

In another part of the sky, a different helicopter soared southward. King piloted while Earl, his companion, browsed a newspaper's 'HELP WANTED' section. "You don't suppose he really is coming up here, do you?" King asked.

Earl merely shrugged in response. King pressed on, "Well, I'd say the good old boys have had it coming to them for quite a long time now, wouldn't you?"

Earl circled an ad, distracted, while King voiced his worries. "We're not going to lose our jobs, Earl. We're too good at what we do. Don't worry."

Suddenly, a deafening 'WOOOSH' cut through the air, followed by the roar of thunder. The helicopter jolted, King momentarily losing control. "What the hell was that?" he exclaimed.

Earl pointed down, spotting the jetfoil below and the State plane above it. Another 'WOOOSH' sounded this time from the jet chopper zipping past. King regained control of the helicopter, turning it around to pursue.

The chase was on. Helicopters and planes scrambled, vying for position. The aircraft darted around, trying to surround the jetfoil, which persisted in its path, evading their efforts.

Suddenly, a jet boat burst onto the scene. Frank, at its helm, managed to pull up alongside the jetfoil. The Flying Princess II sharply turned, almost capsizing Frank and Jessica aboard the jet boat.

"This is crazy, Frank. Don't!" Jessica yelled.

But Frank, determination etched on his face, zipped ahead, prepared to try again.

Inside the pilothouse, Myron peered nervously out the window, his eyes darting in every direction.

"Down!" he ordered.

"But they're right underneath us," the captain retorted.

"I said down."

With a deep breath, the captain yanked the height control lever.

· · ·

Beneath the jetfoil, the waters churned with added intensity. The vessel surged forward, picking up speed. The ensuing spray engulfed Frank and Jessica, leaving them spat out and completely drenched.

"Still think he loves you now?" Frank shouted over the roaring water.

Jessica's voice trembled with exasperation. "Oh God, why me?"

21

Myron turned his attention back to the captain, his expression intense. "It doesn't feel any lower."

The captain shrugged. "Can't tell. Computer control."

Frustration was evident in Myron's voice. "Where's the border?"

The captain pointed off in the distance. "The lighthouse. Right up ahead."

Determination flooded Myron's features. "Okay. You just make sure that we get there first. Computer control, my ass!"

The waters were a whirlwind of chaos. Planes, cutters, helicopters, and the persistent jet boat scrambled, attempting to intercept the jetfoil. However, the agile vessel danced around every effort to thwart its path.

Growing impatient, Earl decided to escalate things. He took aim and fired his gun at the pilothouse.

Watching the scene unfold, King mused aloud, "There must be a simpler method of getting that money. If only I could think of it." The entire group was on a collision course with a massive tanker.

Inside the passenger cabin, the passengers tried to distract themselves. A deaf man looked at his wife as they completed a survey. "I put smooth for the ride. What did you put?"

She glanced away, feigning indifference. He strained to hear her response, "Pardon? What was that?"

"I haven't decided yet," she huffed.

As the flotilla veered dangerously close to the slow-moving tanker, its Japanese crew gathered on the deck, waving their arms frantically, trying to alert them to the imminent danger.

Somehow, the collection of vehicles managed to skirt around the tanker just in the nick of time. Helicopters wove patterns in the sky while cutters jostled for space around the jetfoil. Amid the mayhem, the jet boat almost succumbed to the wake.

The passengers already rattled, tried to settle back into their seats. The woman snatched the pencil from her husband's grip, scribbling angrily on the survey. "Rough. Very rough."

"What did you say?" he asked, genuinely not hearing her. Exasperated, she smacked him on the side of his head. To her surprise, he beamed. "I can hear again!"

As they approached the lighthouse, which stood proudly on a rocky point, the flotilla pushed harder, each trying to reach their destination first. The air was thick with tension, gunshots ringing out, and seaplanes diving daringly close to the water. Yet, as they neared the border, a sudden silence engulfed them. The police and the Coast Guard began to drop back, seemingly ensnared by an invisible net. This international boundary kept nations separate. But the jetfoil, the jet boat, and a lone helicopter pushed on, breezing through the unseen barrier.

Rose's fingers tightly gripped the microphone inside the jet helicopter as he called out, "Chopper to Ace plane. What happens now?"

Ace's voice crackled from the other end, "Get the RCMP on the horn. Tell 'em what they've got coming through."

Below, the jetfoil, a sleek embodiment of speed and might, charged toward Victoria. King and Earl hovered menacingly in the vicinity. Swooping in, they unleashed a barrage of shots, causing the windows of the jetfoil to explode inwards.

King's face contorted with worry. "No, Earl. I don't think this will do at all. I do not think so at all."

But Earl, driven by unspoken determination, let out another fiery blast.

Inside the pilothouse, shattered glass carpeted the floor. The captain winced in pain as blood oozed from a wound on his arm. Myron's calm demeanor began to crack. "Keep flying. Come on. Fly," he urged.

Jessica scaled over the transom on the jetfoil's starboard side with agile movements. Frank held onto the boat, keeping it pressed against the foil. Using all his strength, he grabbed the rail and hoisted himself up. Jessica reached out, pulling him the rest of the way.

Together, they sprinted through the passenger cabin.

"Oh, look. Newlyweds. How cute," remarked a woman as they sped past.

Another inquired, "Where did they come from? They're all wet."

A third woman chimed in, giggling, "Honeymoon, dearie. Honeymoon."

Upon reaching the pilothouse door, Jessica pounded frantically. "Myron? Myron let me in. It's me, Jessica."

Inside, Myron seemed to shut out the world. Ignoring Jessica's pleas, he continued to shoot at the menacing helicopter hovering nearby.

Unimpressed by the scene below, King, back in the helicopter, turned to Earl, asking casually, "Pass me the sports section, would you, Earl?"

Distraught, Jessica whispered to Frank, "Frank, they're shooting at him. He can't get out."

"Come on," Frank responded, leading the way. They maneuvered along the upper rail of the jetfoil, dangerously close to the pilothouse. Taking a chance, Frank clambered over the railing.

"Frank, you'll kill yourself!" Jessica shouted, panic evident in her voice.

Frank, not breaking his concentration, muttered, "Thanks a

lot." His heart pounding, he took a daring leap, landing on the roof of the forward cabin. He began sliding, barely holding on with his fingernails.

Inside the pilothouse, the captain's face turned paler by the second as he clutched his bleeding arm. "Fly this thing, dammit," Myron barked. But it was too late; the captain slumped, unconscious. Myron's eyes darted to the co-pilot, demanding, "You. Take over."

Frozen in fear, the co-pilot hesitated. That split-second was all Myron needed. He knocked the man out, took control of the helm, and muttered defiantly, "I'll do it myself."

The helicopter circled for another pass, showering them with more glass. As Myron struggled with the controls, he caught sight of Jessica outside the door, her eyes shimmering with tears. He pulled her inside, attempting to pilot the jetfoil himself.

Tears streaming down her face, Jessica asked, "Myron, what's happened? Why are you doing this?" Myron remained silent, concentrating on the console.

She tried once more, her voice choked with emotion. "I love you, Myron. I want to help. Please, let me help. You need counseling."

Ignoring her, Myron touched a lever, banking the foil. Holding onto the money tightly, they ventured deeper into the channel. "You know how to fly this thing?" he asked. Jessica said, "No."

"Then shut up!"

<h1 style="text-align:center">22</h1>

I n the Victoria Channel, the posted speed limit read 10 KPH. Nevertheless, the jetfoil ignored the restriction and zipped through the water, its powerful engines leaving a turbulent wake behind. Sailboats and motorboats scattered in its path, desperate to avoid a collision with the speeding craft.

Frank, clinging precariously to the roof of the jetfoil, managed to latch onto a window. With great effort, he shoved his head inside, his face a mask of terror.

Inside the pilothouse, which resembled a disaster zone, he cried out, "Stooooop! You got to stop. Tell him to stop, Jessica. We're heading right for the dock."

Jessica looked at Myron, her eyes filled with desperation. "I can't. Myron, please. Listen to me."

With a far-off look in his eyes, Myron held the money tightly with one hand. His other hand gripped the control.

Jessica's voice was tinged with sadness and confusion. "Please, let me help you. Why are you doing this? Why?"

Impatiently, Frank snapped, "Don't ask stupid questions, Jess. Just help me find the button that turns this thing off."

Near the dock, a veritable army of men worked feverishly to clear the streets and divert traffic. RCMP cars skidded to a halt near the pier, officers jumping out to take control of the situation. They ordered boats out of their slips while bewildered tourists scrambled for safety. Another group, weapons ready, took positions on the pier. They were prepared for whatever was coming.

The jetfoil continued its relentless charge, with just a thousand feet separating it from a catastrophic collision.

Inside the passenger cabin, pandemonium reigned. Men ducked, children darted around in fear, and amidst the chaos, a particularly vocal woman lost her wig and screamed, "We're going to crash! We're going to crash!" The co-pilot, eager to stifle her panic, clamped a hand over her mouth.

Yet, within the pilothouse, a deceptive calm prevailed. The digital display showed 50 mph and counted the remaining distance: eight hundred feet, seven hundred.

"Myron. Don't. Please," Jessica begged. In response, Frank frantically pressed every button within reach.

Jessica continued her plea, "I can help you, Myron. It will be just like before."

As the distance closed to six hundred feet, Frank attempted to wrestle the throttle from Myron's grasp, but Myron remained immovable. "Jessica. Help me," Frank implored.

Suddenly, Myron leveled his gun at Frank. "You started this. I'm going to finish it."

Horrified, Jessica gasped, "Myron."

The digital counter continued its relentless countdown. Five hundred feet.

Frank backed away, his hands raised. "I didn't. I didn't start. You—We're just old friends."

As they neared the four-hundred-and-fifty-foot mark, Jessica screamed, "Myron! No!" At four hundred feet, Myron fired. Frank crumpled to the floor. Jessica lunged at Myron in a split second, landing a kick that doubled him over in pain. To her relief, Frank was only momentarily stunned and managed to pull himself to his knees, unharmed.

Outside the pilothouse door, the co-pilot pounded desperately.

Inside, Frank lunged for the throttle, trying to stop the craft. He jiggled it, but nothing happened. In a panic, he exclaimed, "It doesn't work. We can't stop. I'm getting out of here."

From beyond the door, the co-pilot's voice rang out, "The red button! The red one!" Frank scanned the console in desperation with only three hundred feet to go.

"Jessica, Jessica! The red button. Where is it?" Frank shouted.

Flustered, Jessica cried out, "Which one?"

"Which one?!" Frank exclaimed in disbelief.

In a final act of desperation, he slammed all the buttons.

Suddenly, the jetfoil's foils retracted, and the craft splashed into the water with a massive "WHAP!"

The entire dock area was drenched with a sudden spray. A money pack, presumably thrown from the force of the jetfoil's impact, ricocheted off the roof. It split open upon landing, releasing a flurry of bills immediately caught in the fierce wind. They floated about in the air, creating a surreal, confetti-like scene. Soon, the bills were sucked into the rotor of the hovering helicopter, getting shredded in the process.

Inside the helicopter, King's frustration was palpable. He slammed his fist on the dashboard. "Bloody hell, Earl! Now, why didn't we think of that?"

Earl, seemingly entranced, could only watch the floating money, captivated by the surreal sight below.

King continued with a hint of sarcasm, "What we need now is a vacuum cleaner, but a butterfly net would certainly do." He paused, hearing something. Turning his gaze outside the window, he was met with the sight of two police helicopters rapidly approaching.

A realization hit King, and he quickly snatched the paper away from Earl. "I wonder if they have take-out for cosmetic surgery. Something quick and cheap."

Earl, looking distressed, pointed at the incoming police.

"Don't worry, Earl," King quipped. "We can always get you a job as a translator." With that, he pulled hard on the collective, the helicopter veering away with the police helicopters hot on their tail.

Back at the dock, the jetfoil demolished its intended target. The police forces on the ground were prepared, standing at the ready, their focus undeterred even as the escaped money danced whimsically through the nearby trees.

Inside the pilothouse, the hum of the jet engines began to whine down. A hand reached hesitantly for the fallen gun.

Myron managed to pull himself to his feet despite looking shaken and in pain. Frank was sprawled out, seemingly unconscious, while Jessica slowly disentangled herself from him.

"I don't like what you just did," Myron said, his voice dripping with menace.

"I never expected you to," Jessica responded, her tone defiant. "I don't like what you did either."

"It wasn't my fault."

"You tried to shoot him."

"He wanted the money."

A hint of desperation entered Jessica's voice. "Don't I count for anything?"

Nearby sirens screamed, interrupting their exchange. Myron's gaze shot outside, seeing a veritable army of police officers, their rifles aimed squarely at the pilothouse. Panic set in. He grabbed Jessica, pressing the gun to her head.

"Myron, what are you doing?" she whispered, her voice trembling with fear.

"Don't be scared, Jessica. Basil will help us now."

Suddenly, Frank began to stir, groggy from his brief blackout. As Myron and Jessica moved, Frank reached over to shake the jetfoil's captain, who slowly came to.

Outside on the jetfoil, Myron and Jessica were moving slowly and carefully, making their way toward the stairs by the dock. The police officers kept their rifles trained on Myron as he covered Jessica's mouth, holding the gun tightly to her head.

However, an RCMP officer, clearly in charge of the operation, began issuing commands. "Lower your rifles. Let the man through — everyone!"

The main street had been blocked off by the police, creating a clear path. With Jessica as his reluctant shield, Myron began to move past a London double-decker bus. The crowd stunned into silence, watched with bated breath as the desperate man made his escape.

23

Across the manicured lawn that stretched out in front of the Empress Hotel, Myron moved swiftly, dragging Jessica along with him, the cold steel of the gun pressed tightly against her temple. Frank raced after them, anxiety and panic evident in his voice.

"Jessica? Jessica?"

She glanced back, her eyes pleading. "Frank, let me handle this. Please."

Frank hesitated, but the police cleared a path for him, allowing him to keep pace with Myron and Jessica. Her eyes, already shimmering with unshed tears, finally spilled over as the reality of the situation crashed down on her.

"Myron, I love you," she sobbed. "You have to let me help. Please, Myron. Please? I don't understand why."

"Basil will understand," Myron murmured, a desperate edge to his voice.

Frank closed the gap between them by now, but the police were getting restless, ready to intercede. "It's okay. It's okay. Everything's fine. I'm with them. Jessica?"

"Frank. Go away. Leave us alone," she shot back, her voice filled with fear and frustration.

"With him? Are you kidding?" Frank couldn't hide the incredulity in his tone.

She spun around, her eyes blazing with anger. "You're so selfish you don't even know what love is, Frank," she declared before turning to Myron with a gentler tone. "Myron? You're a star. We have friends. They can help."

Frank hesitated, torn between his feelings for Jessica and the dangerous situation unfolding before him. The palpable pain of his love for Jessica was evident to anyone who looked his way. He seemed to know he'd lost her.

Inside the Grand Empress Hotel, a path was hastily cleared for Myron and Jessica by the police. Elderly ladies pressed themselves against the walls, eyes wide with terror. Frank called out to her not far behind, "I do know. I care about you, Jessica. I have for years. I won't give up on us, Jess... ever."

The echoing footsteps of tourists were interrupted as they stepped out of the way. Jessica's voice quivered as she spoke. "Myron, listen to me. When this is all over, you'll be better, and we can still get married just as planned. I love you, and I want to help you."

Frank, watching the scene unfold, slowed down. "Jessica? I'm leaving. I'm going now, just like you asked. I'm going... goodbye..."

But she seemed lost in the moment, her attention fixed on Myron. As Frank made his way out, he crossed paths with Ace, a sardonic smirk on his lips. "Gonna have a hard time getting all that money, aren't ya?"

Ace's reply was swift, "We don't need to. It's fake."

Frank's laughter was hollow. "Oh, beautiful."

"I switched it in Monterey. Standard procedure," said Ace.

Frank couldn't help but grin. "Lucky you."

He took off, leaving the scene behind as quickly as possible.

In the conservatory of the hotel, a space that once housed clandestine meetings with Basil, Myron looked around frantically. His face contorted with rage when he realized Basil wasn't there. "Where is he?"

The room, filled with murmurs just moments before, went deathly silent. An RCMP officer dismissed a brave waitress who had stepped up to Myron, and soon after, Myron's resolve seemed to break. Tears welled up in his eyes, and he relinquished his grip on the gun. Ace made his presence known, flanked by more officers. As they took Myron into custody, Jessica's voice was filled with disbelief.

"Why are you doing this? What did he do? He didn't do anything. They took his kids!"

Her pleas were met with silence from the officers. When she sought answers from Ace, his revelation was chilling. "Jessica, no. Myron kidnapped his own children."

"But why?"

"He needed the money. He owed a lot of people," said Ace.

Jessica's world seemed to crumble around her. "Myron? Your very own children? Is this true? Did you?"

As Myron was led away, lost in his own world of regret, Jessica clung to him desperately. "Myron didn't know. He couldn't have known he was hurting them. I'm sure. He's too kind."

Ace's voice was gentle though firm. "I'm sorry. Myron and I have a few things to talk about. Quite a few things."

"You're not going to hurt him, are you? We were supposed to be married today. I just needed to be with someone like him," she said in a low voice.

Left in the center of the bustling room, wearing her soiled white wedding dress, Jessica looked heartbreakingly vulnerable. Her voice barely more than a whisper, she called out, "Frank?"

But he was gone.

The night sky was full of stars, a brilliant celestial canvas that served as a backdrop to the vibrant sounds of youth and energy. Cheers erupted from a crowd, mostly in their twenties, happy and full of life. An amplified voice filled the air above the stage at the Greek Theater.

"Hello there! You're looking great!" Frank's voice rang out, and he dazzled the crowd, his charismatic energy infectious. Confident, one year later.

"I hope you're having a good time!" he shouted, and the crowd went wild. They loved him, every word and every note.

"Two, three, four—" he counted off, and the band started up. Thirty pieces strong, the music soared, a backup singing trio danced nearby, and the stage came to life.

Frank began to sing, his voice rich and soulful.

The crowd milled about the box office, buzzing with anticipation. Jessica pushed her way through, eyes alight with purpose. She reached the window, where a sign announced: FRANK CORBIN - SOLD OUT.

"Are there any tickets left?" Jessica asked, hope tinged with desperation.

"If there were, I wouldn't be sitting here," the ticket lady responded, not lifting her eyes from her magazine.

"What about tomorrow night?"

"Tonight's the last night. Sorry."

Disappointment washed over Jessica's face. She had aged noticeably. The past year had not been kind to her. Just as she was about to turn away, a seedy-looking guy approached her.

"You want a ticket? Fifty bucks," he said, showing her a crumpled ticket between his fingers.

"I don't have that much," Jessica said, stepping back.

"I wouldn't say that," the man replied, grinning as he looked her over.

Unsettled, Jessica pulled away from him, blending into the crowd until she was just another face—lost but hidden.

Frank reached the edge of the stage, belting out a beautiful song that echoed through the theater. But suddenly, he stopped. The band kept playing, but Frank doubled over in pain and dropped the microphone. One of the singers rushed over to help him.

"What's wrong?" the singer asked.

"I'm sick," Frank said, his voice strained.

They hurried off stage while the band played on, leaving the crowd murmuring in concern.

In the dressing room, a swarm of people hovered around Frank—arrangers, composers, managers, photographers, publicists, singers, and friends. Danny, the only familiar face in the room, pushed through the crowd to reach him.

"Frankie, what's the matter? You sick?" Danny asked, concerned, etching his features. Frank nodded. "What is it? You want a doctor?"

"No," Frank replied.

"I don't want you to conk out on me now. You got stuff to do. Gonna close tonight. Put you on tour in Europe. You gotta record an album in London next week. You can't just conk out on me now," Danny said, frustration building.

"Who are all these people?" Frank asked.

Danny looked around at the faces. "They're making the arrangements for you, remember?"

Frank just stared back at him, drained.

"All right. All right. Everybody out. We need some air here. Frankie's gotta breathe," Danny ordered, and the room emptied. From beyond the door, they could hear the crowd shouting for Frank.

"They're not gonna let you get away with this. They paid good money, and they wanna see you finish," Danny said, turning back to Frank.

"I'm tired, Danny. I never see the same faces anymore. Just yours," Frank confessed.

"Yeah, well, I got a good face. There's not a lot of faces you wanna look at for more than ten minutes, you know," Danny quipped. "So, what is it? What's wrong? You got everything you need right now. Cars, money, girls. All of it. Tell me. What's missing?"

Frank took a long time to answer, but Danny waited. "It's lonely here, Dan. It's probably lonelier at the top."

"That's why you're a performer. That's what it's like," Danny said, almost defensively.

"But I just don't know if it'll last," Frank finally confessed.

"Oh, that. Just nerves. It's biological," Danny said, pacing the floor. "It's that girl, isn't it? All year long, that's all you talked about is that girl. I don't know why you never just called her."

But Frank was already at the door, on his way out. "Hey? Frank, you gonna be all right? Frank?" Danny called after him, but it was too late. He was gone.

Back on stage, Frank bounced back into the spotlight. The audience erupted in joy. "They're telling me that we have to cut it short tonight 'cause it's supposed to rain," he announced.

Boos and no's filled the air from the crowd in the open-air amphitheater.

"But if you can sit in it, I can play in it," Frank countered. The crowd cheered him on; their mood flipped as quickly as a switch. He cued the band, and they began a slow tune. He sang his voice a sweet ache in the night.

Meanwhile, outside the venue, student sentries patrolled the area with flashlights and guard dogs. People were backed up three deep outside a chain-link fence. Every now and then, someone would muster the courage to climb over. Most were snapped up by the dogs and thrown out, but Jessica was watching and learning. A whole group tried overpowering the patrol. Half made it; the other half scattered.

Emboldened, Jessica started to climb. Her sweater tore on the fence, but she pushed on, adrenaline fueling her every move. She made it over and headed down the aisle, her heart pounding.

Along a dimly lit aisle, Jessica hurried towards the stage, her heart racing and the echoes of Frank's voice guiding her path.

As the song's intensity built, Jessica drew closer to the stage. But her pursuit didn't go unnoticed. A couple of sentries spotted her with their barking dogs and began to close in. Her breath quickened, her feet nearly tangled beneath her, but she persisted, desperately trying to reach the stage.

Frank continued, oblivious to Jessica's plight.

But as the sentries finally caught up with her and the dogs lunged, Jessica's scream pierced the night, "Frank? Help me!"

24

___

On stage, Frank's attention was immediately drawn to the commotion. His voice faltered momentarily as he caught sight of Jessica. He sang, paused, and sang, but his eyes locked on Jessica.

"Jessica?" he called out, panic evident in his voice. "Hey! Let her go. That's my best friend. Let her come up here."

As the sentries reluctantly released her, Jessica staggered onto the stage. Frank quickly approached her, shielding her from the eager gaze of thousands.

"Have I got something special for you!" he exclaimed to the crowd, a mischievous twinkle in his eye, "... and it ain't my nerves."

Holding her hand, he leaned in, his voice just above a whisper, "What are you doing here?"

"I'm sorry. I had to," she replied, her voice trembling.

"What took you so long?" he teased before addressing the crowd again. "You're gonna love this! Jessica Blair, folks, is in the house."

The audience clapped.

Jessica hesitated momentarily before admitting, "I had to feel it for myself. I had to be sure."

Frank's gaze softened, "This is Jessica Blair, and we're going to do my favorite duet for the first time... and properly." He whispered to her. "Are you free?"

She could only nod in response, overwhelmed by the moment's intensity.

Frank gestured for one of the background singers to approach, "Tell Danny two tickets to Europe. I've decided to go. You like Venice?"

Jessica's eyes widened, her mouth dropping open in surprise.

Reveling in the anticipation of the crowd, Frank cheered, "Okay, here we go."

But as the band began to play, Jessica hesitated, her confidence wavering, "I'm nervous."

"What? Stage fright?" he asked. Frank tried to reassure her, "What about me? How do you think I feel? Look at my knees shake."

The song's poignant lyrics continued, and Frank sang his part, soulful and with heart. "Come on. It's your turn."

With a deep breath and after tender coaxing from Frank, Jessica found her voice. The crowd watched in rapt attention as the duet unfolded, a true testament to their connection and the power of music.

Frank and Jessica's voices harmonized perfectly, filling the atmosphere with palpable emotion.

"And I love you every day, and I love you every night. So, this love's for you." He waited, coaxed her, and smiled. Then Jessica sang. "This love's for us."

And together they sang. "This love's for us wherever we are. No planet, no place, nothing is too far. -- This love's for everything we do, this love's for you."

Together, they sang, their voices weaving together seamlessly.

Frank looked deeply into Jessica's eyes, the weight of the moment settling upon them. Jessica's voice, filled with emotion, echoed his loving line.

Frank's gentle and insistent voice sang again. Their voices came together once more in perfect unison. "This love's for you."

Then, with the final note still hanging in the air, they drew closer, their lips touching, then kissing passionately.

As their silhouettes intertwined, the starry night above reflected the romance between them.

REVIEW

If you liked this book, please fee free to leave an honest review. Thanks so much.

http://www.amazon.com/review/create-review?&asin= B0CHDGF6QW

ALSO BY A.C. JETT

- ALL BOOKS
- A Warm Winter Chill
- <u>Abduction</u>
- The Albatross
- The Architect
- Bad Brakes
- Calabasas Hills
- Crash Site
- Desperado
- Earthlight
- Fast Track
- <u>Final Appeal</u>
- Gideon's Fault
- Hal, The Spud King
- Healing Time
- Heartstorm
- High School
- Hypocrisy
- Identity
- Nefarious
- One More Time
- Powder Stream
- Red Ink on Steel
- Sense of Duty
- Shadow Run
- Special Feature Live!
- Stage Fright
- Star Children
- Wanderlust

- Warm Body

RED INK ON STEEL

The hot California sun bore down on Chuck Chasem, a thirty-five-year-old undercover private eye threading through traffic on his beat-up Harley Davidson. With his tanned skin and lean physique, he was an odd sight on this tar-sticking-to-the-tires kind of day, clad in tennis whites that bore a single black tar stripe on the back. The roar of heavy metal music echoed from his biker radio, nearly drowning out his self deprecating thoughts..

My name is Chuck Chasem. I'm an undercover private eye. I used to be a tough, big-city cop. Now I'm insecure, he stated in an almost resigned tone.

A black Town Car attempted to squeeze him out of his lane with an aggressive honk, but Chuck retaliated with an extended middle finger.

Before I went solo, I had a big office with lots of staff. Gave that up a long time ago. Who needs the hassle of an address when your cases sometimes take you on the wrong side of the law? His hand reached for one of two cellular phones attached to his handlebars, dialing a number on instinct. A woman's voice babbled on the other end.

"Yes, honey, no, honey. Yes, honey. No. Honey. Honey, what makes you think I'm patronizing you? I'm just calling," he responded, navigating around a pickup truck bearing a barking German Shepherd. The near miss earned a harsh insult from Chuck before he reassured his phone companion. He spotted a speed trap ahead. "Jerk! No, not you, honey. Some guy with a dog. Not your dog, Tramp."

In a kitchen in the city, Melanie, Chuck's twenty-three-year-old girlfriend, was elbow-deep in the process of making a meal. The fun-loving brunette dealt with a spill of thick red sauce on her blouse, a scene watched by her Doberman, Tramp, seated in a high chair, bib and all.

"Tramp? Who are you calling a tramp?" she questioned her attention on the phone.

"Not Tramp, honey. Trap. It's a trap. A trap is what I said?" Chuck tried to explain, his voice maintaining the cool he'd established.

"No. No one called. You've got nothing going on. Oh, and Chuck. Your report is brilliant. Almost too brilliant," Melanie responded, skimming through his thick report even as Tramp attempted to clean the sauce from her blouse with his tongue. She ended the call, leaving Chuck on the freeway, staring at the cloudless sky.

Why the hell not, huh? Don't people know I'm the best damn cop this side of Amsterdam? he mused. His thoughts were interrupted by a white Wagoneer pulling up next to him, driven by a blonde so young she looked fresh out of high school. Their eyes met, and she winked. As Chuck's phone rang again, he shifted his attention back to the road, taking the call.

"Chuck Chasem here. Your problem is my opportunity," he answered, sliding into his business persona.

"I need a good dick. I hear you're the best," the young woman from the car, Delaney, responded, her voice teasing.

"You've been talking to my press agent. What's the case?" Chuck inquired, his gaze returning to Delaney's car as she answered.

"It's my father. He says someone's trying to kill me," she stated matter-of-factly.

"We better meet," Chuck suggested.

"Dinner, Mateo's, eight, She proposed before hanging up.

"How will I know you?" he asked.

"Can't miss me. I'm fun," was all she offered.

Chuck watched as her car pulled ahead, the license plate reading '976FUNN'. The black Town Car he'd noticed earlier slipped past him to follow her.

Minutes later, the freeway was gridlocked with stalled traffic. Chuck found himself alighting from his bike to relieve himself at the side of the road, effectively blocking a car. The irate driver honked at him, but Chuck continued his phone conversation.

"I thought you were playing tennis," his mother's voice drifted from the other end, clearly puzzled.

"Cover story. I was disqualified," he retorted nonchalantly.

Simultaneously, his mother, a healthy-looking woman of fifty-five, was tending to her garden. She was busy pulling weeds out from her vegetable patch and disposing of the garbage.

"Why?" She asked. His voice echoed in her ear, telling her, "Can't discuss that, Mom. It's classified."

"Well, dinner's at eight and your sister's in town. You can tell us the whole story then."

"Wouldn't miss it for the solar system." Chuck said.

He abruptly ended the call as the traffic started moving again and zipped up.

Climbing back onto his Harley, he was met with a dead starter. His attempts to jump-start the bike only led to burnt knees from the exhaust pipe and a flat rear tire.

Frustrated, he gave up and removed a chicken leg from a saddlebag. Munching on it, he stuck out his thumb to hitch a ride just as an ambulance and two highway patrol cars passed him.

With a sinking feeling, Chuck jogged to the accident site, where two highway patrol officers assessed the scene. He gnawed on a greasy wing and tossed the wet chicken bone into the cop's front seat. An officer of size, George, was visibly irritated to see him.

Delaney's white Wagoneer, lay upside down, clearly totaled.

"Lost control, huh?" Chuck quipped.

"Low flying bird, Chuck," George replied. .

"Must have been huge," Chuck joked.

"We think it was a flock."

"Any frame damage?"

"That would complete the picture," George smirked.

Chuck took a closer look and noticed the vanity plate – '976-FUNN' - now bloodied in the grass. He picked it up. The steering wheel spun in the back seat, and a front axle break seemed too neat, almost deliberately cut.

"Too quick for me, George. Busted axle, looks like. Radio work?" Chuck casually inquired, inciting a sarcastic response from the officer.

"Why, you want to steal it?"

"Can't hock a broken one."

Paramedics began loading the beautiful Delaney onto a stretcher and into the ambulance.

"Poor girl," George said.

"We were supposed to have dinner tonight."

"Guess you got to find yourself another victim."

A tow truck driver, Susan Cage, a muscular, sweat-drenched, tattooed woman of fifty, sauntered over chewing on a rusty nail.

"Hey Chucko, what are you doing here?" She asked.

"Car wreck. Kind of a hobby of mine."

"Some hobby."

"It's the only one I got."

"That's a crock."

Cage spat out the nail and pulled a fresh one from her greasy pocket as she unfurled her tow chains.

"So that's how you keep that perfect figure, dieting?"

"Get lost." Cage grabbed a tire iron, headed menacingly toward Chuck.

The paramedics started to close the ambulance door.

"Hey, you think I can hitch a ride with you guys?"

"A friend of the family?" The paramedic asked.

"I can be." Chuck unlocked the door, dove into the ambulance and turned to Cage. "Say, let me know when you wear out that training bra." He winked.

"Eat shit, Chucko," Cage replied as she threw a tire iron at him. The ambulance took off.

Red Ink on Steel